The Canary

The Canary

A Novella

Clint Haugen

Clint Haugen

This book is dedicated to you, me and everyone else.

But there are a few people I have to personally thank. Lauri Bonn slashed this book red several times for me. She believed in me, and in this book, when she had no reason to. I am forever grateful, Lori Bonn. You can slash me red anytime.

Jennifer Ball and Hannah Winishut, your feedback, enthusiasm, and direction were invaluable to me. This book is also dedicated to you two as well.

Life conspired against me to create this. It flowed out from some place that is still confusing to me. This book is dedicated to life, as well. Whatever that means.

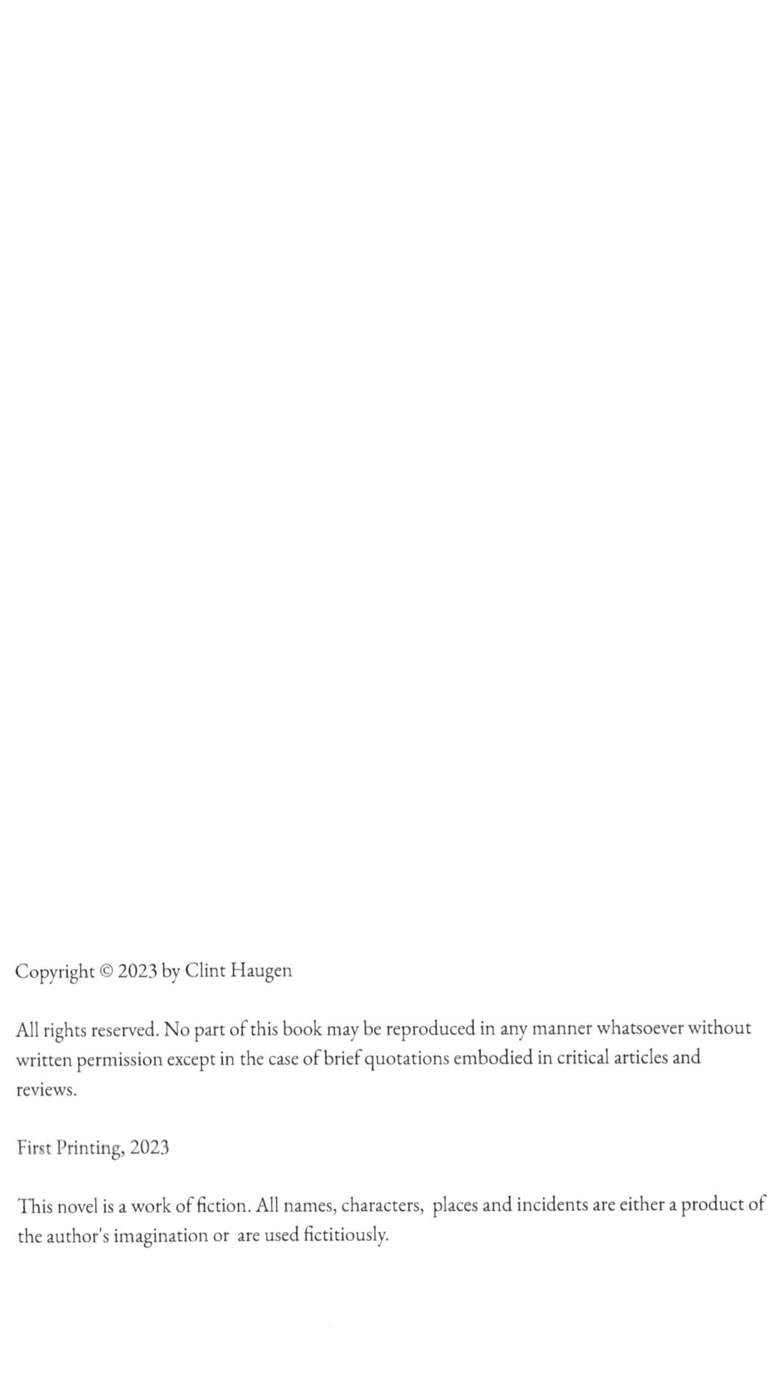

"Hey, Doc. How's it hanging?"

"I'm doing well—thank you for asking, Owen. It's been awhile since our first session. You're letting your hair and beard grow out, I see. It looks good. Very biblical."

"Biblical?"

"Yes, Biblical."

"You mean the western version of those characters? I'm starting to look like them?"

"It was just an observation, Owen. No need to get defensive already."

"I've missed you, Doc. You're a real gem. You know that, don't you? You, with your fancy shoes and nice family. Such a good American boy you are. I bet you've never gotten in trouble in your life. I bet you view yourself as a peacekeeper. 'Doing the Lord's work' is what your wife calls it, huh? Yeah, she does, doesn't she? Ha. Well, bless you, Doc. Let me sit back and take life advice from a man who's never struggled with money a day in his life. You're a man who's never missed a meal. But go on, tell me where I'm broken. Tell me about me. Please, Doc, go right ahead."

"Are you done?

"You're doing that thing again where you turn everything into a fight. Remember what we said, 'Leave it in the gym.' Conversations are not competitions. You cannot win them."

"I bet you're fun at parties, aren't you? I bet you talk about your fancy car and the problems with the modern man, as you sip on an expensive whisky. You talk shit about your coworkers and friends, just to fit in, don't you? You shoot longing glances at your friend's wife, as your wife flirts with the most exciting man she can find. And you both pretend like you don't notice the other, don't you?"

"You know I don't have to do this. I am here for you, but I don't have to take this. I am not your verbal punching bag. I am your doctor—"

"—You're a doctor like Dr. Pepper is a doctor."

"You don't respect my education?"

"There are lots of bad doctors out there. Just because you went to college and charge up the ass, that doesn't mean you're a good doctor."

"No, it doesn't. You're right about that. There are bad doctors out there. I can't deny it. Therapy is about having someone to talk to. It's about human connection. Having a good rapport with your therapist is all that really matters."

"Sure, Doc, whatever you say. Listen, when a surgeon makes a mistake, there will be physical evidence of that mistake. But when a psychologist makes a mistake, it's the psyche that suffers. And that suffering can manifest itself in more issues that the psychologist has to address. Therapy can be a perpetual spiraling of bullshit if you aren't careful."

"Is that why you're so resistant, Owen? You think this is a 'perpetual spiraling of bullshit?' And you think I am 'a doctor like Dr. Pepper is a doctor?'"

"Well, you make me sound like a real ass-hat when you say it like that. But yeah, essentially that's what I am thinking."

"Well congratulations. You've won the fight. I'm done doing this with you. I am tapping out. I am no match for you. You clearly have it all figured out. So you don't need me. Sounds like you just need yourself. The only thing I'd like to know, Owen, is why did you schedule this session today?

"Owen?

"Take your time."

"Because I need more than myself.

"I need other people . . .

"I don't have anything figured out.

"I'm a mess, Doc. And I try to hide it from everyone. I try to be strong, but sometimes, I'm not. Sometimes I feel weak. I feel broken. But no one wants that; no one wants a weak and broken man. No woman does . . . and I don't want to be alone, so I hide it all. I tuck it away. Deep down, behind the soul . . .

"Have you ever cried in front of your wife, Doc?"

"Well, let me think . . . only once I guess."

"Why were you crying?"

"My father had just passed."

"And after you cried about your father in front of your wife, how long after that did she wait to fuck you again?"

"What the fuck, Owen?!"

"How long??"

"Well, I've never thought about it before. But now that you brought it up, I think it was six months later."

"I'm sorry, Doc. That's rough. Women aren't really attracted to vulnerable men. That's what they say they want, but really, so many of them don't know what they want, and as a result, men don't know what to be. Sensitive sometimes, but strong and stoic the rest of the time? That's not how emotions work. We can't just flip a switch and be someone else. Don't you agree, Doc?"

"Well, not exactly, but . . . You know, I was 33 when my father passed. She and I were in our sexual prime right before that day. I mean, we were freaks man, freaks. She liked to be tied up and blindfolded, and she—Uh, you know, never mind. But now we don't even talk."

"Oh shit. Y'all are divorced then?"

"Yeah—ten years today, actually."

"Fuck, Doc, I'm sorry, man. You still love her, don't you?"

"Always."

"I'm sorry about what I said earlier, Doc; I've just been in a mood lately."

"I can tell. You came out swinging today."

"So you never had any kids then?"

"She never wanted any. But now she's remarried. Four kids. Every time I see her post a picture of her kids and family, a part of my soul burns away."

"That's poetic, Doc, I am going to steal it."

"We've gotten way off topic. I apologize, Owen. I got distracted and unprofessional."

"I feel like we are making great progress though. I can relate to you so much more now that I know you've suffered a little."

"It's unprofessional to talk about our personal lives with our patients."

"You got to talk about it with someone, Doc. You got stuff tucked away under your soul, too."

"Everyone does. Even the women who have seen us cry. They have stuff tucked away, too. And most don't try to show it—they try to be strong. But when they show it, it is no big deal to us. We love them and comfort them. We feel that we can only show our pain from our suffering at the bar, in therapy, or through our art. That's what you do, Owen. You use art to process your thoughts and emotions. Your poetry is your therapy. And you also use the bar. But what is it you are always saying, 'We don't have an objective lens to look at ourselves through. The ruler is trying to measure the ruler. We need other people to help us see ourselves.' You don't get that through your art, do you?

"Owen?"

"You've read my writing?"

"Of course.

"Owen, is everything alright?"

"That shit is personal, Doc. That was a huge invasion of privacy."

"You're quite talented."

"You really think so?? Well thank you, Doc. I'm trying.

"So you think I need you? You think I need an unbiased third party to help me see myself? A more objective lens?"

"Yes, I think that, and I know that you think that too. Or does your philosophy apply to everyone else and not yourself?"

"Yeah, yeah, I see what you're saying Doc."

"You're very intelligent, Owen, but even the most intelligent of us know almost nothing. 'The fatal flaw of the western man is the ego. His hubris haunts him, preventing him from growth. The death of the first ego is the birth of a worse ego.' Take your own advice, Owen."

"Quoting me back to me is the most annoying version of therapy that you've tried. And I know that I know nothing. Or, maybe I don't know it? I learned that from Mr. Hemlock himself . . . But maybe I didn't learn it? Whatever, it's confusing, Doc."

"You already know all the answers, Owen. I am just here to help you see the questions a little differently."

"Alright, Doc, we'll make this a weekly thing for a while. Do me a favor though?"

"What's that?"

"Don't read my writing."

"Fair enough."

"Later Doc."

"Have a good week Owen."

"So, see you at the pub then?"

"No, Owen, you won't see me at the pub."

"Sure, Doc. Sure."

2

"Heya, Doc! How's it hanging?? I like the scruff, Doc. Looking very hipster, my guy. I like it. Anyways, what's new?? What's going on? I missed you at the pub last week. I was keeping an eye out for you."

"We need to have a serious conversation, Owen."

"It's always a serious conversation with you, man. Never any fun. Let's have a drink. Do you have booze here?"

"No, Owen, I do not have booze here. And this is what I need to talk to you about. We need to set boundaries. I am not your drinking buddy. I am your therapist."

"Yeah, man, so I know what I want to talk about today."

"Oh yeah? And what is that?"

"Love."

"Love?"

"Yes. Love."

"Well, what about love do you want to talk about?"

"How do you do it?"

"How do you do love?"

"Exactly."

"Can you elaborate a little more?"

"I know how to love people in a general way, you know? But being in love—that's not something I feel very good at. It feels too irrational. Too chaotic. It hurts so much, Doc. It shouldn't hurt this bad, it shouldn't, doc. I'm doing it wrong. I have to be. Love shouldn't hurt this bad, man. It just shouldn't."

"Sometimes it does, Owen."

"And we are just supposed to eat it and move forward?"

"What else can we do?"

"Shit. I don't know Doc! That's why I am asking you!"

"I do not have your answers for you, Owen. Everyone loves differently. I can only listen and try to guide you along your own journey. But, please tell me more about your hurt."

"It hurts, Doc."

"What does?"

"Love.

"It has always hurt, Doc. Every time I fall in love, it hurts. It's usually a few very brief moments—too brief, if I am being honest, and then, so much hurt. I don't think any one of them, for even one moment, loved me back."

"Do you think any woman has ever loved you? Maybe your mother? She loved you, didn't she?"

"Yeah, in her own fucked up way she did."

"What was her fucked up way?"

"She was a hardcore smother-mother for way too long. She's definitely got a personality disorder or two. And she has to try to convert me to Christianity every time I see her. We don't really talk anymore."

"When do you think you started to resent your mother's love for you?"

"Well, I don't know if I would say that I resent her love . . . but maybe around 16."

"What happened around age 16 with your mother?"

"That was when my parents got divorced. But maybe it started earlier . . ."

"And how did their divorce make you feel?"

"I had to sit in the courtroom. I was the only one of us kids who had to do it. I had to listen to my parents rip each other apart over money. They were animals, Doc. Savage animals. And then, at the end, I had to decide if I wanted child support from my dad or not. I chose not to. I ended up living with my dad instead of my mom. We lived in a one bedroom shack next to the high school. It was a dump. It had no heat and I had a bed in the kitchen/living room. I think that's when my relationship with my mom really started to go downhill.

"She really knew how to manipulate men.

"The household was crazy toxic for the few years before their divorce.

"They both had some real intense moments with my older sister when she was a teenager. But she was off at college battling her own demons to see the worst of it.

"And their fights were so intense. I remember, as a child, they would scare the shit out of me. The fights between my mom and dad, I mean. Their fights with my sister were fucked up sometimes too, but the ones between the two of them hit deeper.

"My younger brother lived with my mom most of the time after the divorce."

"How did your parents divorce affect your brother?"

"I don't really know."

"You guys never talked about it?"

"I guess not."

"That's probably something you two should have discussed. You live with him now, right? How's that going?"

"Good. We've always gotten along. I wish he would help out with my dog more, though. I hardly see him. We have opposite work schedules. And the house is kind of divided. I'm upstairs and he's downstairs, so even when we are home together, we aren't together. He was going through a rough break-up, remember? I told you about it before—the first time I was here?"

"Oh yes, that's right. Have you talked to him about seeing a therapist?"

"Uh . . . no, I have not."

"That's probably another conversation you two should have."

"Yeah, probably . . . "

"So your mom was the first love you knew from a woman. What about your second?"

"Alex? Yeah, she was great, but that hurt."

"Why'd it hurt?"

"We were good friends for a year before she and her boyfriend broke up. He was a state champion wrestler, who had a notoriously giant penis. And he was the nicest guy. She and I had one summer together, spent under the stars."

"Then what happened?"

"Then she started talking about how she was going to move to a city 150 miles away. I got scared and pushed her away. She never moved and ended up back with her ex. I held onto those feelings for her for way too long. And then I ended up fooling around with her best friend, Jazz. I lost my virginity to the best friend of the woman I loved, on her couch, in her apartment. I lasted two pumps and sat with my head in my hands afterwards. I'll never forgive myself for how I made that angel feel about the sex afterwards."

"You mean Alex's best friend?"

"Yeah, her. She was so good to me back then."

"Did you ever talk to her about it?"

"I don't think so."

"Did you ever talk to Alex about it?"

"I don't think so."

"Well . . ."

"Yeah . . ."

"That sounds like some unresolved trauma, Owen."

"I've played those moments with Alex over and over again in my head.

And same about the moments with Jazz."

"How old were you?"

"I was 18."

"What about your sister? How was your relationship at that time?"

"She had a breakdown at college. She was misdiagnosed with bipolar disorder when she was 18 . . .

"Doc, they put her on medication that made her spirit disappear.

"That's one of the reasons the fights with my parents were so intense. Imagine being 18 and you're told that you have bi-polar disorder?

I am pretty sure something happened while she was at college. I think it was sexual assault, maybe rape . . . I'm not sure."

"You've never talked to her about this?"

"No."

"Owen."

"I know, Doc! I know!

"I guess I don't talk to people about things."

"You're talking to me now and that's a start."

"A start?"

"Do you want to change, Owen?"

"What?"

"Do you want to change?"

"Listen, Doc, our time is up. I have a date in 20 minutes."

"A date? Are you excited?"

"Not really. See ya, Doc."

3

"Aye, Doc! What's crappening?"

"Oh, you know, same shit, different day."

"Holy shit, Doc! I've been saying, 'what's crappening' for ten years and no one has nailed a response like that! Bravo sir."

"It was too easy, really. You lobbed it up for me. It was low hanging fruit. My mother used to say that I would make a great stand-up comedian."

"My mother used to say that I'd make a great pastor."

"Mother's can be funny, can't they?"

"Sure, Doc."

"Have you thought more about forgiving your mother since the last time we spoke?"

"Is that what you wanted me to get out of the last conversation?? Sheesh Doc, I thought you were saying that I should hit up Alex and see what she's up to.

"I'm kidding, Doc. I knew what you meant . . . I almost did hit her up though. She works with raptors now. Pretty fucking bad ass if you ask me. And she has a Carl Sagan book I want to borrow. *The Pale Blue Dot.*"

"So you don't want to forgive your mother? You're still holding onto the past?"

"The past is what has made me, Doc. I forgave my mom for most of the childhood stuff a while ago. It's the present one that I have issues with."

"How so?"

"She keeps asking me to go to church with her. She uses her birthday and mothers day as leverage, thinking it'll sway me to go. But it hasn't worked in four years. I don't want to go to church with her and she doesn't respect that. She tries to manipulate me, Doc. She always has."

"What's wrong with going to church every now and then? A little coffee, community, a little singing, and some philosophy. What's so bad about that?"

"I think you mean mythology, Doc, not philosophy."

"Maybe there is both in the Bible?"

"I don't want to play pretend for a few hours so my mom can look good in front of her church friends. I'd never ask her to stop being a Christian for me, so why should she ask me to pretend to be one for her?"

"You can't set aside your ego for a few hours in order to make your mother happy?"

"My ego? I don't want to fake it for her. I shouldn't have to fake it for her. She shouldn't ask me to do that."

"I see your point, Owen. And you seem to be pretty stubborn on this one, so we can drop it for now."

"I know you're a man of faith, Doc. Listen, it doesn't bother me. I know that there are good and bad people that take part in every belief system, every philosophy, and every political party."

"Well, I am glad it doesn't bother you. But would it bother you if I said that I truly believe the answer to most of my patients who are going through a crisis of meaning, is faith?"

"Faith in God?"

"Faith in anything."

"You're right, Doc, I am stubborn about this one. Let's drop it for now, like you suggested."

"Okay, Owen. Last week we were talking about love. Shall we pick up there?"

"Sure."

"We talked about your mother's love and the love you felt for your friend, Alex. Should we talk about the next time you fell in love?"

"Sure, if you want, but there isn't much to tell because I never told her how I felt about her."

"How come?"

"I guess . . . I was afraid to.

"Hey, Doc, I think we need to call a play from Freud here, and talk about sex."

"Oh really? Why sex?"

"Because it was after Alex that the meaning of sex got really distorted for me.

"I thought that the key to keeping a woman was good sex."

"Oh boy."

"I know, Doc. And I was incredibly insecure about my sex game."

"Oh. What did you do? Wait . . . you thought that you had better get good at sex, so when the next woman you really cared about came along, you'd be able to keep her?"

"Good lord, Doc! You're really nailing it today!"

"Good lord?

"Figure of speech . . ."

"So?"

"So, I had sex with a lot of women."

"This tracks . . ."

"It was 'practice' for me. And it was fun sometimes. But . . . other times, I was embarrassed about how long I'd last . . ."

"You could've used a therapist back then."

"Yeah, no kidding."

"How many women?"

"I have no idea."

"Seriously?"

"Super cereal, Doc."

"Wow. Do you think sex is a problem for you? How has it been for you lately?"

"Grab some popcorn, Doc, this shit is about to get good."

4

"Hello, Owen."

"Hey, Doc. Do you think I can stretch while we talk today? Do you have a foam roller?"

"No, Owen, I don't have a foam roller here. But you're welcome to stretch. Are you tense?"

"Tight."

"Where are you tight?"

"Everywhere."

"Have you been training again? Or are you still out with your knee thing?"

"Still out. Somehow sitting around at home makes the body feel worse than getting the shit kicked out of it. The body is weird that way, huh?"

"Are you sure it's your body—and not your soul—that you're feeling?"

"What do you mean?"

"You love doing martial arts. You had dreams about being a great fighter. It was your passion for ten years. When you train and fight, you are feeding your passion—you are feeding your soul."

"Yeah, I understand you, Doc. It does feel like that, and without it in my life, I feel lesser. I feel like I am missing a piece of my soul. If I didn't have the other parts of my soul in my writing, my guitar, and my books, I think I would've died a while ago."

"Died?"

"Yeah, Doc, died."

"How would you have died?"

"There would've been no place for my soul to go. My whole identity was wrapped up in being an elite fighter. That's how I was going to get respect. That's how I was going to show my friends and family that I've been working hard towards a goal. That's how I was going to make money. It was all of me. It was my only plan. They say you have to burn the boats to be great at something. That's what I did, Doc—I burned the boats, and the bridges, and all of my time. I burned my shoulder, my hamstring, my nose, my hand, my back, my knee, everything, Doc! I gave all of myself to that dream. I lit that passion up. Just for two or three moments as an amateur.

"My soul would have fizzled out if I didn't find The Artist."

"The Artist is you?"

"It's one of my alter egos."

"Are you a superhero, Owen?"

"Nah. I am a villain. Who sometimes does nice things for the people he cares about."

"That doesn't sound very villainous to me."

"The Artist thrives in the chaos, Doc. So does The Fighter, but that's a different kind of chaos. The Fighter battles an external chaos, while The Artist is fighting the internal chaos."

"Very interesting . . .

"Battling the chaos sounds like the motivation of a hero to me. Why don't you see yourself as the hero, Owen? That's how most individuals see themselves these days."

"'The hero myth.
The land of the free.
But not free to be me.
The west, where we are better than the rest.
The hero myth grows and grows and grows—
all these individual heroes make up this *home*.
America is a big reflection of ourselves,
and instead of ourselves staring back,
we are shocked to see Narcissus in our eyes.
But the hero myth gets retold,
stroking the fragile ego
of the American made narcissist.'"

". . . Did you just quote yourself?"

"That was a freestyle, Doc. Off the top. It wasn't my best work, so I won't charge you for it."

"How kind of you.

"So are you afraid of becoming a narcissist? An 'American made narcissist?' That's why you don't want to view yourself as a hero?"

"Doc, I know that you know that I am at least a little narcissistic. I mean, aren't we all? So many of us just want to be seen and heard . . . I just don't want to get any worse. I don't want to feed The Narcissus in me. I want to starve him."

"Is The Narcissus another one of your alter egos?"

"He lives with them. I just try not to use him. He and The Judge are good friends. They want me to be perfect."

"You sure have a lot of characters in that head of yours. Are there any more?"

"Sure, there are a few more. There is The Child, The Philosopher, The Lover, and The Alchemist."

"Huh, you've already taken a few therapeutic principles and applied them to yourself . . . Almost like Yung's archetypes. It's interesting. Not sure if it's healthy, but . . . And you've been using these 'characters' in your writing?"

"They've been using me, Doc."

"How curious."

"So what do you think are some of your narcissistic qualities, Owen? It's not as common as people think. An actual narcissistic diagnosis is rare."

"I'm so introverted these days, Doc. Everything I do is for me. I wanted to be a great fighter for myself. I wanted to be a writer for myself. I am learning the guitar for myself. I work out for myself. I read for myself. Hardly any parts of me lay inside other people. I've split my soul up and put them in ideas, in potential; personal potential and ideas about what I could become. I fell for the American myth, 'If you work hard enough, you can achieve anything.' But that's not true, is it? Sometimes you work incredibly hard and the universe doesn't reward you. Life isn't fair that way, no matter what the myths say. I am a product of my environment, Doc, and this environment is full of individual, narcissistic, pleasure-seeking zombies. But here's a question I want to ask you. How do you become aware of how bad your narcissism is? Like how much should I be focusing on myself and how much should I be focusing on others?”

"First, I think we need to work on shifting your perspective about your fellow westerners. 'Individual, narcissistic, pleasure-seeking zombies?' That's a bit harsh, don't you think?”

"Is it, Doc? I can't tell anymore.”

"I think that if you give some of your soul to other people, they'll give you some of theirs in exchange. It might not always be an equal ratio, though—keep that in mind. Sometimes you'll put all of your soul into someone and they won't give a shit about you, but other times, someone will put their whole soul into you and it'll be beautiful and terrifying. You have to try, Owen. You have to try with them.

"And secondly, we know how bad we are through the eyes of other people. They reveal to us who we are. This is why relationships are so important. We need people who will love us enough to call us out on our bullshit. We need partners who will relentlessly support us, but also challenge us in the areas we need to be challenged. That's how we grow. Healthy relationships are our antidote to narcissism. This is just one of the reasons why we have to make an effort with other people and our relationships. You have to try, Owen.”

"I am trying, Doc . . . I am trying.

"You and I are both villains in someone else's story . . .”

"What? Who said that?"

"I did . . .

"I wrote it a long time ago . . ."

5

"Do you think you slept with all those women because you were missing the love that you rejected from your mother?"

"Sheesh, Doc, I just got here. Not going to ease me in at all today? You need the foreplay, Doc, you can't just thrust right in. I was going to tell you about this dream that I had."

"It's your session, Owen. We can talk about whatever you want to talk about."

"Are you okay, Doc? You seem a little off today."

"I haven't slept much lately."

"What's going on in that graying dome of yours?"

"Well, I'll just mention this briefly, then we'll focus on you. Deal?"

"You really need to open up more, Doc. It's not healthy to leave it all bottled up. Let it out.

"Do you want to switch places?"

"If you are going to make a joke about this session today, we can cancel it. I'm tired."

"It's foreplay, Doc! Just foreplay! Let's hear about these dreams."

"For the last few months I have been having nightmares about getting old and dying. I know it's normal to start having these dreams at this age, but I can't get myself to stop the nightmares, no matter what I tell myself, or who I talk to."

"A few months, Doc? That's a long time to go without good sleep."

"I hardly sleep. I just stare at my ceiling fan, watching it spin around over and over again."

"Have you tried weed?"

"What?"

"Weed. To sleep."

"I get paranoid. Getting high makes my anxiety worse. It's probably not a good solution for you either, Owen."

"Do you always get paranoid?"

"Always."

"Huh. Well it helps with my sleep.

"What about booze? Have you tried that?"

"I am a sad drunk. I put on Johnny Cash and try to remember happier times."

"Are you afraid of death?"

". . . Yes."

"Well there's your problem, Doc! Wait. Don't you believe in an afterlife? Shouldn't that comfort you as you get older?"

"Lately, I've been having doubts."

"Doubts about God?"

"Yes. Doubts about God."

"Good lord, Doc! This is serious. When did the doubts start?"

"A few months ago."

"When the nightmares started?"

"Yeah, around the same time."

"What about God are you doubting?

"Doc?"

"I'm only going to talk about this because I think it might help you."

"Sure, Doc."

"I've believed in God for most of my life and I've tried to be a good man. I've tried to live a life that God would be proud of . . . but what's the point of living a Godly life if I feel like this? I know all the tricks to fool the psyche, but these doubts have been haunting me. I furiously hold onto my old beliefs. I don't know if I should let them go . . . or double down. I don't want to die feeling like this."

"Virtue is its own reward, Doc."

"What?"

"Virtue is its own reward. That's what one of the Stoics said. I'm pretty sure it was one of them. You live a good life based on the standards that you choose, so you can look at yourself in the mirror and be proud of who you are. It's not easy to be virtuous and the universe may never pay it forward, but we do it anyway because it's the right thing to do. It's a good model for little boys and girls. Whatever we wish the world to be, we must first be it ourselves."

"Maybe we should switch spots, Owen?"

"I'm going to lay on the floor, Doc. I hate sitting."

"You're one of my most difficult clients. You know that, right?"

"What? I feel like we are having a great time!"

"You control where these conversations are going. You deflect when something gets difficult and try to get me to talk about my life instead. And then you psychoanalysis me.

". . . This isn't right."

"Sorry, Doc, I didn't realize that's what I was doing."

"You have a micro understanding of psychology and you think you can play psychologist with me."

"A micro understanding?

"Maybe you're right, Doc. We all seem to have a micro understanding of the psyche these days, and we love to take that micro understanding and diagnose ourselves—and everyone around us —with these 'conditions' we don't even understand. But Doc, I'm just trying to help you sleep. I'm worried about you."

". . . It's not me you should be worried about. Have you had any of those conversations with the people we've discussed? Have you forgiven any of them? Have you practiced any of the tools we've worked on? Has this done you any good at all?"

"I don't know, Doc . . . I feel lighter after coming here. The spirit feels lighter, you know what I'm saying?"

"You need to try to be a student here, not the teacher."

"Sure, Doc. I'll try."

"I get carried away with you. It's my fault too. I have not been a good therapist to you. I've been distracted lately . . ."

"I disagree. You're doing fine, Doc. Don't sweat it."

"You need better help than me, Owen . . .

"So, tell me about this dream."

"I had sex with Scarlett Johanson in an elevator that was stuck on the 13th floor!

"It was wild, Doc. I picked her up and pushed her up against the wall. Her ass kept hitting the buttons with each thrust. There were cameras recording it all. A sex tape was released a few months later and I became rich because of it. Scarlett moved in with me and we popped out a kid. She was so sexy, Doc. So sexy."

". . . I don't think I am going to dive too deep into the meaning of that one."

"You should try having dreams about her. I bet you'd sleep a lot better if you did."

"Owen, there's something I want you to practice, if you're willing. I think it might really help you."

"What am I supposed to practice, Doc?"

"Trusting women."

"Dude, are you serious?"

"Absolutely. I am assuming you're familiar with exposure therapy, dude?"

"Yeah Doc, I am. When I was 19 I self-diagnosed myself with Atychiphobia. I thought that was why I was laying around smoking weed and watching shows all day. I thought that I was afraid to try. So Doc, I picked the hardest thing I could think of to do, and tried it. It just took me five years to get in an actual gym and six years to step into a cage, but I overcame my fear of failing. I slowly exposed myself to my fears and started to believe in myself again. I shadow boxed and worked out alone for 10,000 hours before I became confident. You see, Doc, I thought I failed royally at being an athlete in high school. It was my whole identity and I was so lost without it. But worse than that, I was scared to try at anything. It was a deep fear. But I willingly exposed myself to it and became someone else. I had a dad who had tremendously high expectations for my athletic career that never happened, and a mother that tried to make me afraid of everything in the world but God. But she also made sure that I was terrified of him, too. Well, I felt stuck after high school. But I grew. At least, I think I did. At least, that was the idea. Now I'll try anything. That's why I recklessly write and throw it out there for the world to see. I don't have the fear of failing. Now I have the fear of not trying. I turned my lead into gold, Doc. But now I think that I misdiagnosed myself with Atychiphobia back then. Most of us are terrified of failing, aren't we? It's more of a natural human condition than anything else. I think we all must take ourselves through exposure therapy at times, Doc. That's how we grow. We have to fail."

"Very impressive Owen, but I think there is an even deeper fear that you now must willingly expose yourself to."

"And what's that?"

"Love. You must face your fear of rejection and learn how to love. You'll have to take a leap of faith some day and trust women again. But listen Owen, start slowly. And for the love of God, don't just pursue sex."

"Okay, Doc, I'll try."

6

"Aye, Doc! I have to tell you about this new dream I—"

"Owen, I want you to meet Dr. Sara Greene. She's here to observe our session today."

"Hello, Owen. It's nice to meet you. I've heard a lot about you. Don't worry, I don't bite. I'm just here to observe."

"Hey, Doc, what's this about?"

"Dr. Greene has agreed to observe us today. Nothing for you to worry about. Take a seat, Owen, or do you want to lay down on the floor?"

"Actually, I think I'll stand today.

"So are you observing me, or the Doc?"

"I'm just here to listen. I'll take a few notes, but it's best if you and I don't interact. Pretend I am not here."

"Is she serious, Doc?"

"Yes, she is serious. You're pacing, Owen. It's okay. Why don't you talk about why Dr. Greene being here makes you anxious."

"I'm supposed to pretend she isn't here, and honestly talk about her?"

"You can't do that?"

"Not honestly.

"You gave her my file?"

"Yes, I did."

"Isn't that, like, illegal?"

"This is a special case, Owen."

"A special case? Me? Above the law? Above my consent??"

"It's technically not illegal."

"Technically? What the hell?"

"We are exploiting a loophole."

"I think that's all we need to tell him."

"Yes, that's all you need to know."

"Man, Doc, I don't know how I feel about this."

"Tell me about those feelings."

"Well, I was just really starting to vibe with you. I think we can relate to each other on many levels. We are making progress together. So I don't know why we are throwing a wrinkle into this."

"This is only for today. After this session, it will not be like this."

"Er, okay, I guess."

"So Owen, are you ready to begin?"

"Sure."

"Do you want to take a seat now?"

"No, I'm good standing."

"Okay then. If that's what you want. Why don't you tell me about your week?"

"I just worked. That's it. Nothing exciting happened."

"How's work going?"

"It's so boring, Doc. I'm losing my mind there. I just want to fight, write, fuck, and play the guitar."

"Maybe it's time for a change in your professional life. How's the resume?"

"I haven't looked at it in seven years."

"Might be time to update it. What do you think?"

"Do you really think a new job will be less boring for me?"

"Depends on the job. You need something challenging."

"That's what writing, fighting, and playing guitar are for."

"But those don't pay bills. It's great that you have your passions, but you need stability too."

"I like chaos."

"Maybe update the resume. Think about it at least. If something feels off, we need to acknowledge it, and then come up with a plan on how to deal with it."

"Yeah . . . maybe."

"How's the writing going?"

"I'm hoping to put out a few books soon. Some poetry, some fiction, some philosophy, and maybe a script or two."

"Wow, that's a lot. That's great news. What's your plan?"

"Plan? I've already written most of it all. Just have to polish up a few things and I'll be good to go."

"What about publishing? How're you going to do that?"

"I've heard self-publishing is the way to go these days, but I haven't really looked into it. I just like to write. The marketing and publishing are things I'm not good at. I don't have the time or energy for all of it."

"Well, Owen, if you are going to self-publish and make money, you better start thinking about those things."

"Yeah."

"Do you have any money saved up for publishing?"

"I did. But . . . I spent it on a gift."

"A gift for who?

"A woman?"

"Yes."

". . . Her? The woman you are in love with? The one we talked about during our first session together? The reason you started to come to therapy?"

"Yes, Her."

"Have you given it to Her yet?"

"No, the artist is still making it."

"The Artist?"

"No, not him, an actual artist."

"I see."

"I'm thinking about telling Her that it's for Her dog, not for Her."

"Why's that?"

"I've gotten insecure."

"How come?"

"She doesn't give a single fuck about me."

"You know that for sure?"

"I'm pretty sure."

"Have you talked to Her about it?"

"Nope."

"Are you planning on it?"

"Nope."

"Well, something else to think about."

"Hopefully that conversation doesn't happen anytime soon, Doc."

"Why's that?"

"I'm terrified."

"Of the hurt?"

"Yes, Doc, terrified of the hurt."

"How's it feeling now?"

"It hurts."

"Are you still chewing your lip?"

"Yes."

"What about your muscle spasms—still having those?"

"Yes."

"Above the heart?"

"Yes. And in the eyelids."

"Have you seen a doctor yet?"

"You know I don't trust doctors, Doc."

"But you trust me?"

"I mean . . . I was starting to."

"Well, as someone you once trusted, I advise seeing a doctor about your muscle spasms."

"Sure."

"So, Owen, I'm thinking about taking some time off from my practice."

"I figured it was something like that. Why else would she be here? There's no loophole like this. Are you my new doc?"

"You can call me Dr. Greene, and yes, I think I will be working with you from now on. Is that okay with you?"

"Are you alright, Doc? Still having nightmares?"

"Let's not talk about that today, Owen. But I'll be fine. This job can be tough sometimes. I want you to know that I've enjoyed working with you. Be gentle with Dr. Greene, okay? She's very capable of handling you. I have confidence in her. I just wanted her to meet you first before deciding to take you on. And this is one of those rare times where I think a change in perspective might truly be best for you."

"A change of perspective? You mean because she is a woman?"

"Yes, Owen, that's what he means. From the sound of it, our sessions together will be very different. I look forward to working with you."

"Wait, shouldn't I be able to pick my new therapist, Doc?"

"You wouldn't pick anyone. You'd stop coming."

". . . That is true."

"Will you be coming to see me next week, Owen? My office is just eight blocks east from this one. Does the same time still work for you? I've cleared my schedule at this time for you."

"Yeah, I'll be there. I'll try anything once."

7

"Have you ever read the book *Fight Club* Dr. Greene?"

"No, I have not. Why do you ask?"

"Have you ever seen the movie?"

"Yes, once, a long time ago."

"There's this line that they added in the movie."

"Okay."

"It's not in the book."

"I figured that much."

"He's talking to Tyler Durden about marriage and responsibilities, and he says that he is a 30 year old man-boy. Do you remember the line?"

"No, I can't say I do. It's probably been ten years since I've seen that movie."

"Can you relate to that line, Dr. Greene? Do you know what it's like to be a 30 year old male struggling to find his identity in western society?"

"No, Owen, I can't say that I know what that is like. I know what it's like to be a 36 year old female in western society. I can only use my knowledge of the male experience, mixed with empathy and logic, to try to grasp what life is like for you. Do you ever do that with the female experience? Do you ever put yourself in their shoes like that?"

"I think I've done it a few times to the women that I've been in love with."

"Oh, all three of them? And your mother? Your sister? What about all the women you've slept with that you didn't care about —do you think about them?"

"Do you know what year the movie adaptation of *Fight Club* came out?"

"You're deflecting, Owen."

"It was 1999."

"Okay?"

"Do you know what else happened in 1999?"

"No, Owen, I don't. Let's stay focused on empathy."

"Woodstock 99 happened."

"So?"

"If you want a glimpse at the mind of the western man at the turn of the century, take a look at the bands at Woodstock 99. Pay attention to their audience and what happened there. Look at who was the top artist at that time. The top movies. *Fight Club, American Beauty, The Matrix.* That was prime Eminem. Prime Limp Bizkit. Peak Red Hot Chili Peppers. Look at the 90's. We got Nirvana. And look what happened to Kurt. Really look at it! Use your empathy and logic and see what has been happening in the mind of the psyche of the western man! The increase in suicides. The incarcerated man. Mass shootings! The mental health crisis! How can you relate to that? Your lived experience is as a woman. You've lived in a different world than I have.

"Something is bubbling up with men, and no one seems to care."

"He told me that you can get like this. Take a few breaths, Owen.

"I'm glad you got that out. You bottle up those feelings, don't you? You're afraid most people won't understand. A lot of women would jump down your throat and tell you that their 'lived experience' has been tougher than yours, and that you have no right to feel sorry for yourself, but I won't say that to you. Men and women have different obstacles in life to get through. Men have an insane amount of pressure to be providers, although that narrative is shifting, and maybe that's why modern man is struggling to find a solid footing in western society. But let me ask you, Owen . . . When you walk home alone, Owen . . . do you get scared?"

"No. But I am a fighter, I don't fear many men."

"Can you imagine what it would be like to be a woman walking home late at night?"

"Sure."

"Take a second, really think about it. Really try to feel it.

"Close your eyes . . .

"Breathe . . .

"Feel the fear . . .

"Deep Breathe in. Big exhale . . .

"Now imagine feeling like that all of the time . . .

"Imagine being objectified by half of the world . . .

"Take another big breath . . .

"Imagine growing up and everyone in power is a man . . .

"Breathe . . .

"Imagine what it would be like to be growing up and having society pressure you to look and act like an adult, just so they can sexualize you . . .

"Breathe . . .

"Open your eyes . . .

"What do you feel, Owen?"

"Hurt. I feel a sliver of the hurt women must feel sometimes."

"That's excellent, Owen. Neither women or men have it easier than the other. Oppression is not a competition, Owen. All genders, all races, all people have different obstacles to overcome. Navigating through society as a woman isn't easy either."

"I know that."

"But do you embody it?"

"I don't know . . . I try to."

"It's natural to focus on your own experience, but it isn't just an individual subjective experience, is it? There are 7.2 billion other people on this planet. It's a shared experience, Owen."

"I know."

"So are you okay with a woman as your therapist?"

"I might be okay with you as my therapist."

"Well that's something."

"Can I ask you something, Dr. Greene?"

"Of course you can."

"Have you ever had a man cry in front of you?"

"Yes, all of the time. Half of my patients are male. Some cry sometimes. Why do you ask?"

"Do you think a woman wants a man who cries in front of her?"

"I can't speak for all women. And I don't speak about personal issues with my patients. Why does it matter?"

"Well, it's part of this shared experience dynamic, isn't it?"

"I suppose . . . Are you afraid to be vulnerable in front of women, Owen?"

"I'm a poet . . . I know about being vulnerable in front of people."

"What about being vulnerable in your relationships with females?"

"I've only cried in front of a few women . . . I don't think they wanted to fuck me afterwards."

"Fuck you? What does sex have anything to do with this? Not all of your female relationships have to be romantic, Owen."

"Yeah, I know that."

"Do you really?"

"I think so . . ."

"Well, that's our time Owen. I feel like we took big strides today. I'm proud of us. Will you be here next week?"

". . . I think so."

8

"Hey Doc!! What in the hell is going on, man?? It's good to see you! Let me buy you a drink! What're you drinking?"

"Whiskey."

"Whiskey? You sure?"

"Neat. Thank you, Owen."

"Cheers, Doc!

"I knew I'd run into you at the pub some day! I had an intuition about it, I swear! You've got a beard now—are you trying to steal my style? What did you call it? Biblical?"

"Listen, Owen, it is good to see you, but we really shouldn't be talking. It's inappropriate."

"It's fate!"

"Fate?"

"Sure, why not?"

"Why not?

"Huh . . . Okay, well, there are a few things I do want to ask you about. Firstly, why the hell do you call a bar a pub? You're from Oregon."

"I just think pub sounds cool."

"That's it?"

"That's it."

"Well damn. I was hoping for a story behind it."

"Haven't I given you enough stories? Good God man, that's all I do these days!"

"Fair enough.

Okay, second question . . . What do you believe in? We never got around to that."

"I believe in believing. I believe in trying."

"What the hell does that mean?"

"I think we should try to believe in the most magical and beautiful meanings of life. Whatever that is, I believe in it. You see, Doc, I think that the biggest variable that makes up the 'lens' we see reality through, is our beliefs about reality. So, if we do get to choose, and that choice has some influence on my experience of reality, then why not choose the most grandiose magical one? The one full of meaning, you know? And I think we should try to embody that as best we can."

"Then you should forgive your mom for being enthusiastically Christian, shouldn't you, Owen?"

"Hey! Get the hell out of here with that shit, Doc!! No more free drinks for you. I thought we were having a nice conversation at a nice pub, and you turned into a therapy session! Unbelievable. Well you aren't my therapist anymore, Doc."

"I'm just trying to help. My bad. How's it going with her anyway?"

"She sucks, Doc. She's dry. We have no banter; not like you and I had. I felt like her punching bag by the end of it. I felt heavy afterwards . . . but I think we made good progress in a few areas."

"She's just trying to be professional. That's where I fucked up with you. It got too personal. You got to know who I actually am. That's why she had to take you on. I asked her to. I'm sorry if that broke your trust."

"Eh, whatever Doc. Now you're just an average Joe to me and not my shrink. It's better this way anyways. Let me buy you another drink."

"Whiskey."

"Hey, who are you here with?"

"It's just me."

"Really? You got a ride?"

"I can drive."

"Don't be a fucking moron. My date isn't drinking. She can drive you home."

"Your date? Who's that?"

"I honestly don't really know. I don't save numbers on my phone until after the first date. And that's only if we connect.

"We had just gotten here when I saw you. She's over there."

"What's her name?"

"I think it's Ana."

"You think?"

"I don't know man! I've been in my own world today. Let me check my phone, I think she was from tinder. Hold on."

"You're a piece of work."

"Kelley! That's her. 'Likes punk rock. Considers traveling a lifestyle. Is a Sagittarius.' Oof. I don't believe in that witchcraft, but if I did, I would not like Sagittariuses. She enjoys wine, books, and her dog Bubba. Bubba? Poor guy looks like an anorexic squirrel. Okay, this will be easy. Follow my lead."

"What is wrong with you?"

"What do you mean??"

"I'm not going to crash your date."

"Sure you are!"

"No, I'm not."

"Well, you sure as shit aren't driving. Come have a beer with us. Look, she's getting impatient. She's scrolling through her phone. Let's go!"

"So Kelley, this is my friend, Doc. He's very drunk and he is going to hang out with us for a while, and we are probably going to take him home. Cool?"

"Cool with me. What's up dude? So you're drunk? Like how drunk?"

"I'm not that drunk."

"He's hammered. He doesn't normally sound like this. And his cheeks aren't usually this red. See? Red cheeks."

"Will you stop staring at my damn cheeks! I am fine. I can drive."

"No man, I don't think you should."

"See? Kelley thinks so too. Thank you, Kelley."

"So how do you two know each other?"

"We were part of the same theater group growing up. I know he looks old, but he really isn't. He's only halfway to eighty-six. He still has half his life ahead of him, lucky guy. He played Tinkerbell in our play once. His performance was Tony worthy. It really was."

"You should know, young lady, that he's an idiot."

"Oh yeah, I can tell already."

"Well you two are rude. I don't like this ganging up thing. Kelley—you're cut off from drinking for the rest of the night!"

"Okay, not like I was drinking anyways. I had to pick your drunk ass up for our date, or did you forget?"

"Perfect! You stay sober. One of us needs to do it if we want to watch over this guy."

"Yeah, he's an idiot. How do you two really know each other?"

"He was my shrink up until a few weeks ago."

"Really? You go to therapy? That's not the vibe I'm getting from you."

"That's because it didn't work on him."

"You must not be a very good shrink."

"Hey! The Doc is a great shrink! He really helped me understand my sex dreams."

"Well, at least I did something."

"I'll toast to that. Cheers, Doc! Cheer's, Kelley! Pretend you have a cup full of delicious beer, Kelley."

"Wow. I'm babysitting two drunk man-boys. What a great date this is. It's a good thing you're handsome."

"I skate by on my looks and charm. It's true. The world treats pretty people differently. It's a sad reality."

"Relax, you aren't that handsome. Your arrogance balances it all out."

"What? Am I arrogant, Doc?"

"Yeah, you are."

"A wise man can never admit he is wise! If he does, then he is surely a fool!"

"What's that from?"

"I think I made it up."

"He does that. He may be an idiot, but he's a decent writer. I'm not sure drunk free-style ramblings are his best work, though."

"He called me talented once! I heard him!"

"You're a writer? What kind of writing?"

"He does everything."

"Everything?"

"Everything."

"Stop talking about me like I am not right in front of y'all."

"I don't see it."

"He was a fighter once too."

"Once? I still am! I'll kick your ass right here!"

"Yeah, I don't see that either.

"Would I have seen any of your fights or read any of your books?"

"Nah."

"That makes sense."

"You're being real judgmental tonight, Kelley. Typical behavior for a Sagittarius when mercury is out of Gatorade."

"Out of wha– you're into astrology?"

"Only if you are."

"What're you?"

"I identify as a badass."

"What's your sign?"

"It's Gryffindor. What's your sign, Doc?"

"I'm a Gemini."

"Ewww, you're gross. I don't think we should give him a ride home anymore, Kelley. Gemini's can drive drunk for all I care."

"Do we just ignore Owen, or what?"

"Hey, he's your date."

"So Doc, what have you been doing with yourself since you quit your practice?"

"I didn't quit. I'm just taking a break. And I've been doing a lot of this."

"Painting your cheeks red?"

"I don't— . . . yeah, you just ignore him."

"I can't believe you got paid to listen to him."

"It wasn't enough."

"So you've been drinking a lot? What else?"

"I've been reflecting . . ."

"On?"

"Everything."

"I've been thinking about downloading one of those dating apps that you are always on."

"Ha! I'm not always on them! He's kidding. Tell her you're kidding, Doc. What happened to the doctor-patient confidentiality?"

"Which ones are you on? Tinder? Bumble? Hinge? Which one should I get?"

"None of them. Just find a woman you find beautiful and ask her out for coffee. It's easy."

"Kelley knows nothing. Asking a lady out in person is terrifying. You have to do it from your phone, where you are miles away from her. That's the way of the modern man."

"It doesn't seem like you have much to offer a respectable woman right now though . . . Maybe you should wait."

"The Doc has a heart of gold! He deserves someone decent!"

"Maybe he does, but if he wants a kind and intelligent lady, he has to bring something more to the table."

"He shouldn't have to . . . He should be enough."

"He isn't."

"Can you guys stop talking about me like I'm not right in front of you?"

"Sorry, Doc."

"Pull yourself together a little bit and you can bag a nice lady. You got this man. Just comb your hair, trim your beard, stay sober for a few hours, and you'll probably do alright. How's the resume looking?"

"We don't like resumes."

"Well, being employed is definitely going to help."

"She has a lot of opinions for someone who's known us for all of seven seconds, doesn't she, Doc?"

"I think I'll wait to start dating."

"Probably a good call."

9

"Thanks for driving us home. Look, he passed out already. Poor fella. He's really going through it right now."

"I'm taking you guys to my house. You two can sleep there. I'm not driving you two dumbasses all over town tonight."

"So, you're kidnapping us?"

"Yes."

"Well, Kelley, you've caught me at a time in my life when I am supposed to be forgiving to women. So we forgive you. Do you have food?"

"Stay the fuck out of my fridge. I know your kind, they can eat you dry if you let them."

"I did have a roommate call me 'a human garbage disposal' one time. Well, one roommate called me it many times."

"So you're supposed to be more forgiving to women? Is that what your therapist said? Do you have a problem trusting women? Have you been burned before?"

"I don't know how to be in love."

"No one knows how to be in love. And it's not something that you do, it's just something you are in."

"... You know, I paid that guy back there thousands of dollars and he never once said something that profound."

"I'm more than just a pretty Sagittarius queen—I'm smart too."

"I hate that you call yourself that."

"I'll drop you off right here."

"Sorry, Miss Queen. I'm here for your amusement. I can sing and dance, I can play music and tell stories, whatever you need, Miss Wise Sag Queen."

"That's better."

"So how bad of a date is this?"

"I've honestly had worse."

"That's a win for me."

"Do you have roommates?"

"Just Bubba."

"Your anorexic squirrel?"

"I will murder you."

"I bet you listen to those True Crime Podcasts—you'd totally get away with it—am I right?"

"Absolutely, I would."

"How would you do it? Wait, let me guess . . . Poison?"

"Of course."

"'Of course,' she says casually. Did you already think about this?"

"Yes."

"When?"

"On my way to pick you up."

"You thought of a way to murder me on your way to pick me up?"

"Not murder you, just, you know, in case something were to happen."

"In case what was going to happen? Where's the trust here?"

"Like if I thought you were the type of guy to drug my drink at the bar."

"Oh, shit . . . Maybe you aren't a psycho Sag."

"I am just a woman. Sometimes we have to think about getting drugged and raped at a bar."

"I never really thought about that . . . I always thought that two people should meet each other with the intent to trust the other."

"It's a brutal world out there, dude. You have to be ready for it."

"Do you carry a gun?"

"No."

"Why not?"

"I'd accidentally kill myself, or someone else, if I owned a gun."

"Do you know how to throw a punch?"

"I have mace. And this poison I carry with me."

"Shit . . . You aren't kidding?"

"I never kid about poison."

"I can show you how to throw a punch. I can give you lessons."

"Sure, if you want."

"I think every lady should know a thing or two."

"I can play the piano . . . and sing a little."

"You can? That's so cool! I just started playing the guitar. I'm horrible. I'm addicted to practicing though."

"Do you have calluses?"

"Sure do."

"Let me see."

"Yeah, okay. You definitely practice. Would you want lessons on the piano? Can we make a trade-off? Kickboxing for music?"

"Count me in! I've been wanting to learn the piano for a while now. I'm stoked!"

"Well, here is my house. I think we are going to have to carry him in."

"Yeah, he's out. Alright, you get on one side."

"Watch his head!"

"Shit, do you think he is okay?"

"He was a little goofy before, maybe that'll help him?"

"Maybe . . ."

"Okay, one, two, three, you got him? Okay, let's go. Of course you have to make the man walk backwards."

"Are you really complaining right now? I am helping you carry your drunk friend into MY house?"

"Sorry, Miss Sag Queen."

"Don't forget the beautiful part."

"Let's set him down. Do you have your keys?"

"Just lay him down right there."

"Do you have blankets? Don't want the Doc catching a cold."

"Where should I sleep?"

"You can sleep on the floor."

"Perfect. Do you have blankets and pillows for me too?"

"Or you can sleep upstairs?"

"What's upstairs?"

"I am."

"Ohh, I see . . . And what are we going to do upstairs together? Make shadow puppets on your wall? Come up with a dance routine for TikTok? Or tell each other scary stories?"

"You can sleep outside, too."

"Alright. I'm coming. But no cuddling after. Just awkward eye contact and absolute silence. You know, Doc said I shouldn't pursue sex."

"Will you shut up?"

"Yeah, I can probably do that."

10

"She slept with you on the first date?"

"You really shouldn't be so judgmental, Dr. Greene. She is a nice lady."

"Did you persuade her into sex?"

"What the fuck? Persuade her? No. What kind of thing is that to assume? I told you, she invited me up to her room. We left the Doc on the couch. The three of us went out for breakfast together the next morning. Then we drove Doc to his place. He seemed in better spirits at breakfast. It was good to see. I was getting worried about him."

"It was extremely inappropriate."

"That's what he said."

"I doubt he ends up practicing again."

"I didn't like him at first. I thought he had a stick up his ass, but he really is a solid one. Just a little lost right now. Do you have a therapist, Dr. Greene?"

"That is personal, Owen."

"We don't have any banter. It makes this so serious. And boring."

"This isn't one of your dates, Owen. Why do we need banter here?"

"It's seasoning. Just a little spice can make the meal go from bland, to kickin."

"You aren't going to get any 'spice' out of me. I'm here to help you address your issues. We need to come up with solutions for your problems . . . What's funny?"

"The Doc told me that his job was to help me ask the right questions. He said that I already had all of the answers inside my psyche."

"Did that make you happy to hear that you already have all the answers?"

". . . Yeah, I guess it was oddly comforting."

"I'm sure.

"You know I specialize in logotherapy, Owen? Do you know what that is?"

"Yeah, of course I knew that. I did a little research on you. You grew up a middle child to your father, George Greene, and mother, Diane Greene. You graduated from a small high school in Delaware with a 3.65 GPA. Your physics teacher gave you a D- in the last trimester of your senior year. Two years later you accused him of assault. The small town kept it quiet, and the school suspended him for two terms without pay. Nothing was proven. You were going through college. You got into Berkeley, despite the D-, and that asshole. I'm guessing you were too busy at college to take down that guy, but then someone there helped you address your trauma, and you bravely confronted it, just to find out that the system doesn't give a shit about your trauma.

And when nothing happened and the world felt unjust, you got angry and—"

"—that's enough of that, Owen."

"Sorry, Dr. Greene . . . I . . . logotherapy involves finding the meaning of one's life. You asked if I knew what it meant."

"That's not exactly what it means, but yeah, it's along those lines. It's different per individual though."

"Do you know the meaning of your life, Dr. Greene?"

"I wanted to help people that went through trauma, like I did. And I want to find the ones that the system really screwed, and help them."

"Your practice is the meaning of your life?"

"Yes, it is one of my meanings."

"One of them? What're the others?"

"I love to paint. And I love music."

"That's neat, Dr. Greene! I knew there were some layers to you!"

"Sometimes I think about becoming a parent . . ."

"They say parenthood is life changing. I can't imagine . . . They say your meaning changes in an instant. It's kind of scary when you think about it like that. Imagine your life and all you care about changing in just one moment . . ."

"Do you want kids, Owen?"

"I don't know anymore . . . I used to. Everyone from my generation seems to think that it would be irresponsible to bring a kid into this world, but I am not so sure about that . . . I'd settle for a healthy relationship first. And then address those feelings about becoming parents together with my partner when they arise."

"Hmmm."

"Hmmm? What?"

"That's wise, Owen."

"Wisdom is a journey."

"What was that?"

"Wisdom is a journey, without a destination. It's a constant process. It's more like, 'Ignorance is an ocean, and we are drowning in it, and we have to rage against the sea to stay afloat. We have to constantly engage in the process of learning, just so we don't drown.'"

"You look at it like a fight?"

" . . . In a way, I do, I guess . . . A fight that I'll never win . . . But a fight I must fight, regardless of the outcome."

"Hmmm."

"Hmmm? What's with these 'hmmms?'"

"Have you ever felt like your passion for fighting comes from a place of dominance?"

"Yeah . . . I thought about that."

"And?"

"One of my old teammates—just a 20 year old kid—dressed up in tactical gear, armed himself from head to toe, and went inside a Safeway. He killed two people before he killed himself. His manifesto said that he had intentions of going down as one of the most notorious mass shooters of all time. When I read his manifesto . . . I saw a kid who got lost in the chaos. He was scrambling for control of something. He was broken. Defeated. He saw life as torture. It was heartbreaking . . . I thought long and hard about how he used martial arts to let out his violent feelings. Fighting was him flirting with the chaos. That event made me reflect on myself, and why I do it. And no, it's not to dominate someone else. It's not furiously grabbing a hold of some feeling of control. Martial arts is an art to me. It's about the spirit, challenge and problem solving. It's about pushing myself beyond my limits. It's about being proud of myself. It's my art."

"You don't want some control?"

"I've embraced the chaos."

"I don't know what that means."

"I try to let go of as many of the things that are out of my control as possible— which is pretty much everything."

"Stoic philosophy?"

"Yeah, sort of. I want to embody being calm in the chaos. I try not to get stuck in the web that is our projected order on the chaos. Our structures of society are sandboxes that were made for us to play in. Understanding that most of life is out of our control . . . There is freedom in that. Flowing with the chaotic disturbances in our order and routines helps me with my anxiety."

"Is that what you were talking about last time? The issues in the mind of the man at the turn of the century? Men are losing control, and some young men are trying to take it back through power? Whatever power those small men can muster? They are raging against the shifting of power dynamics?"

"Something like that . . ."

"But that's not you? You're on the outside, looking in?"

"None of us are on the 'outside,' Dr. Greene. This life is a shared experience. You said that."

"I did. You're right.

"Just as long as you know you are part of the same people you try to help. Their problems are your problems too."

"Do you know that, Dr. Greene? Are my problems, your problems? Is this practice not an attempt to grab a piece of control over something? People give you control over their whole psyche. They ask you to help steer their ships. Is this not a way for you to . . . dominate men?"

"When you deflect, or try to project something onto me, that's when I know we are really getting at something. You have an itch, Owen. I'm just trying to help you scratch it."

"You're right, my ass does kind of itch."

"What would you say if I asked you to start thinking less in terms of 'Men' and 'Women?'"

"Huh?"

"You see these specific roles in society, 'Men' and 'Women,' but it's 2023—we've evolved past these ideas."

"Huh??"

"Gender, identity, and sexuality exist on a spectrum now."

"Weren't you the one talking about your 'lived experience as a woman' the other week?"

"Yes."

"I have a 'lived experience' as a man. That's how I identify as, and for most of my life, that's how society has identified me. Only in the last five years has society realistically given us more than two options. We are products of our environments, right? I, and my environment, have shaped me as this thing, 'Man,' and as a result, the lens that I see reality through is heavily influenced by this 'lived experience' as a 'Man.' You said we lived in different realities but in the same world? Something like that, right? How shared is my reality with yours?"

"That's subjective—"

"—That's all there is anymore, isn't it? Reality only exists inside my head . . . is that what you're saying, Doc?"

"I'm not Doc. And no, that's not what I am saying."

"Oh yeah. Sorry . . ."

"Did you forget I was a woman for a second?"

"I got lost in the dialectic."

"That's my point, Owen! When real ideas are being discussed, it doesn't matter what gender is discussing them. We can get to a point beyond gender. That's the future; a gender-less society. These traditional gender roles, the way you see the world, it's changing in real time. You have to change too, Owen. Or else you'll get disconnected from reality."

"Yeah, but . . . whose reality?

"Dr. Greene?"

"Yes, Owen?"

"I had another teammate kill himself a few years ago . . ."

"I'm sorry to hear that, Owen. Were you two close?"

"Not really . . . We had the mutual respect that forms when you try to punch each other . . . Dr. Greene?"

"Yes, Owen?"

"People seem to be dropping like flies these days . . . Is this world really THAT bad?"

11

"Getting older is beautiful in its own way. The elderly have survived all the potential accidents, or random failures of the body. They dodged it. They swerved the reaper. I respect them for that. They have been through so much life.

"There's wisdom there, in some of y'all old folks."

"I'm only 43."

"That's the attitude to have! You'll be okay, Doc. I have a good feeling about you."

"You shouldn't be here."

"C'mon, Doc, we are having breakfast! It's my favorite meal! I'm making a scramble, and I'll even let you have some. There's champagne and orange juice in the bag on the counter."

"How do you know where I live?"

"We dropped you off the other night."

"Oh yeah.

"It's eight in the morning."

"Yeah! It is! What're you up to today anyways?"

"It's too early for you. Go away. "

"Did you have another one of your little benders last night, Doc? Another late night with the bottle?"

"You can just leave the food—and the champagne."

"I was thinking about applying for a new job today and I remembered that you also need a new job. I figured we could do it together. Update the ol' resume. What do you say, Doc?"

"It's too early for this. Coffee. I need coffee. Pour me a cup, will ya?"

"But like I was saying, getting older is easy. It just happens. And there is only one thing you can do to stop it. But if you just let it happen—if you don't resist it—it's just like breathing. It's out of our control and we should let it go, don't you think so, Doc?"

"Whoever put the idea in your head that getting older is easy is a fucking idiot. It's one thing to go about life when you're fresh, but it's a whole different experience when everything hurts. Try living when you hardly sleep, nothing excites you, your hangovers last for two days and you have no wife or kids. Try it then and tell me it's easy."

"You're a lot meaner in the morning, Doc."

"How's the writing going?"

"I've hit a bit of a snag."

"What's that?"

"I don't know how to end it. A part of me just wants to let go and have the characters decide."

"What the hell are you talking about? Letting the characters decide? How do 'characters decide?'"

"They just take the story wherever they want."

"But that's you doing that?"

"You wouldn't understand, Doc. You aren't a creative."

"I think you need a shrink."

"I think I am done with therapy."

"Are you sure?"

"Yeah."

"And why's that?"

"I feel good these days. I feel peaceful. Zen. You know?"

"Zen?"

"Yeah. Neutral. I feel calm."

"Even without your ending?"

"Even without my ending."

"Wow. Okay. So no more Dr. Greene?"

"I'm going to break up with her this week."

"I'm sure she'll miss you."

"Do you think I should keep going?"

"I am not really in a place to be giving anyone life advice right now. Do what you want."

"Hmmm. If you say so.

"Listen Doc, in the West we fetishize youth and discriminate against the elderly. We idealize perfection. That's one reason why people feel guilty for getting older. It's not your fault you feel this way. It's very natural."

"Sure, Owen."

"Hey Doc?"

"Yeah?"

"Do you think Jesus is a good person to aspire to be like?"

"Yes, I do."

"But he was supposedly perfect. Is it good to aim towards perfection?"

"He was more than perfect. He was a whole philosophy. A whole movement. Jesus was a whole way.

"He was God, Owen."

"I don't really know what that means, Doc . . . Sometimes I am afraid that our unrealistic expectations for ourselves, and for others, is just self harm. Did you ever feel like you could embody Jesus, Doc? Back when you believed more, did you feel like you could be perfect?"

"No, but I know we all fall short. We know we are all sinners. It's only through the way of Jesus that we can be saved."

"Saved from hell?

"Saved from ourselves."

"Like hell on earth?"

"Something like that."

"Alright, here is your scramble. Eat up. You're a growing boy, Doc. You have to have a solid breakfast. Do you want a mimosa?"

"Sure, why not?"

"So Doc, is having our aim towards an unattainable state of being the best thing for us?"

"What's the alternative?"

"We lower our standards for ourselves, and for other people. We give ourselves more grace in the face of our mistakes. We humble ourselves as humans, not embody Gods. We accept the fact that perfection doesn't exist."

"So we aim lower?"

"We aim realistically. The idea that we have to be perfect in behavior has spilled over into the idea that we have to look perfect too. It's hard to tell where this perfectionism ideal stops, but what if it started with Jesus? And all the demigods, prophets and religions before him?"

"Owen, do you think we are just animals and that when we see a bird swoop up a worm, that we don't feel empathy for the worm, or spite towards the bird, so we shouldn't demonize other humans who do similar things to each other? That's a slippery slope man . . . "

"No . . . I'm just trying to figure this thing out like everyone."

"The idea of being good only finds its legitimacy if there's a purpose for this life."

"A motivation for goodness can't just be because I want to live in a better world?"

"Is that enough of a reason to last you for your life? What if your view on the world changes, will you keep the same belief?"

"Like if I think the world sucks, and there probably isn't anything I can do to change it, what would my motivation be for being a 'good' person then?"

"Yeah, that."

"That's the problem of the modern human."

"It's one of the many problems."

"You know, Doc, maybe it is a good idea to aim dramatically above ourselves."

"Yeah, hopefully . . . It's what I am still holding onto."

12

"I asked for a fight. Just waiting to hear from a potential opponent. 135 pounds. I've been eating cleaner and going on more jogs. I'm stretching more and spending hours alone shadow boxing. It feels so good to have such a clear goal right in front of me. I get focused on it. I laser in—everything else melts away in my life. I can feel something like momentum building up. There aren't a lot of feelings like this one, Dr. Greene."

"Are you nervous?"

"Excited. It's been too long. I've missed it."

"When's the fight?"

"April 4th."

"A little over three months away."

"I asked for a professional fight."

"Wow, Owen, that's incredible. Your first pro fight, isn't it?"

"Sure is. I've been ready for it for a long time now."

"You seem calm. Are you calm, Owen?"

"I have to be the calm in the chaos. I have to willingly walk into violence. It's like driving straight into a tornado, Dr. Greene. It's like dancing with lightning and being as relaxed as you can be. My mind has to be as sharp as my body. I meditate and stretch before bed. It's a whole process, but it almost happens on its own. It's like I just set my sails and let the wind take me wherever it wants. I control as much as I can, and I let go of the rest. It's freeing. When I am locked in that cage, that's when I am really free."

"Owen, were you picked on as a teenager?"

"Uhhh . . . Yeah, a little."

"A little? What's that mean?"

"I think I was arrogant when I was younger. I was asking for it."

"You were asking for abuse?"

"Sometimes I feel like I was asking to be humbled. More than that, I was asking to be hit with the harsh realities of life. I was as ignorant as I was arrogant . . . I'm not sure much has changed . . . I was a soft dreamer. Some of the guys that 'picked on me' were just trying to help me grow up."

"You're defending your abusers, Owen."

"Jesus, or Alyosha would kiss them on the cheek."

"Are you aspiring to be like Jesus, Owen? Are you a follower of Christ now? Or are you trying to be like Dostoevsky's Alyosha?"

"I don't know . . ."

"Is this Doc's influence?"

"I think we are rubbing off on each other in weird ways. He's questioning his faith, and I have questions about faith."

"Do you think Jesus would be alright with you being a fighter?"

"Socrates was a soldier. Plato was a wrestler. Marcus Aurelius was the king of the world, and Epictetus was a slave. If the old testament God does exist, I don't think he cares what we are, just what we do. But Jesus might care about fighting . . ."

"You're searching for wisdom, not God?"

"There is wisdom in religion, Dr. Greene. 'The bible can be both mythology and philosophy.' Doc said that once."

"Why'd you choose a religious man as your therapist? Why Doc?"

"For the same reason you practice logotherapy. The same reason I am sitting here with you now, Dr. Greene."

"Meaning?"

"Meaning."

"Hmmm."

"You and your 'Hmmms,' Dr. Greene. They drive me crazy. So I've been curious, what do you believe in?"

"We won't be discussing that here.

"Hmmm, okay. Fair enough."

"I want to talk about narcissism. Can we talk about that, Owen?"

"Sure. You think I'm a narcissus? That label is pretty trendy these days, Dr. Greene."

"I think you demonstrate a few narcissistic qualities."

"Such as?"

"You have delusions of grandeur."

"Sure."

"You have yourself on a pedestal compared to the rest of us."

"You sure?"

"You loathe yourself."

"Don't those two things contradict each other?"

"Not necessarily. Not if you always fall short of your unrealistic expectations for yourself."

"Hmm, okay, go on."

"You only do things that serve your own agenda."

"Sure."

"You have a need to be in control of a situation."

"I think that one is a miss, Dr. Greene. But one more hit and you'll sink one of my battleships."

"You sleep with lots of women."

"E7? Shit, that's a hit. There goes one ship."

"You're arrogant."

"I feel like you already called that one out. G4? Yep, that was already a hit. Do you have anything else, Dr. Greene? Have you gotten it all out?"

"Gotten what out?"

"You're projecting your issues with the western patriarchy onto me. It's okay, Dr. Greene, I don't mind. You've been through a lot, you can dump it on me."

"Oh, so now you're the martyr? Now you're MY savior? This is typical narcissistic behavior. Can't you see that?"

"Therapy can be a perpetual spiraling of bullshit if we aren't careful."

"No, Owen, you are a perpetual spiral of bullshit."

"Maybe. But is this logotherapy, Dr. Greene? Doesn't really seem like it to me. Seems like this is more Cognitive Behavior Therapy. I do agree with you though. I do have narcissistic qualities. I cannot deny it. I think you are exaggerating a few of the things you listed, and underestimating a few others. But you're in the ballpark. I recently read that narcissists are stuck in the lane of envy. It's a deep sense of inadequacy, isn't it, Dr. Greene? Narcissism isn't arrogance, it's the opposite. It's rocket fueled envy. It's a deep loathing of the self, isn't it?"

"You're educated on narcissism already?"

"Of course. Who doesn't have a few narcissistic qualities sprinkled in their personality, Dr. Greene? I try to recognize mine and starve those qualities. If narcissism exists on a spectrum, I think I am probably in the middle. I am working on moving down the spectrum though. But you missed the best poison the narcissus sips on, Dr. Greene. Envy. Deep, pure envy, that is the root of the modern narcissus. I'm not that. At least, I don't think I am . . ."

"Well, yeah, that is true . . . Some people are more narcissistic than others though, and I think you are the latter, Owen. You should be mindful. You should be careful. Deep envy or not."

"Do you know what it takes to fight another man in your underwear in front of a crowd who wants to see you bleed?"

"No . . . I can't say that I do."

"It takes a delusional type of belief in yourself. The only thing that doesn't make it a delusion is all the hard work that goes into that type of belief. So call me narcissistic. Sure, maybe you're right, but I have to be in order to do what I do. Writing is the same as fighting. I get rejected over and over again. You know not a lot of fans of fighting will talk shit to your face about your fighting skills? It's true—they are afraid of getting hit. But do you know how many people will talk shit about your writing? Too many . . . too many. I want to be one of the greats, Dr. Greene. And you have to sell your soul. You have to put in the 10,000 hours of work. You have to sacrifice everything . . ."

"And what if you lose?"

"I won't."

"You might. Will you develop a deep seeded envy then?"

"What kind of shit is that to say to a fighter before he fights? Do you want me to get hurt?! That's how people get hurt in there, Dr. Greene. They have doubts. I can't have doubts. I have to be focused on one outcome."

"So you're asking me to play into your delusion? As your therapist it's my job to point out your delusions to you."

"Fuck you, Dr. Greene."

"You put so much pressure on yourself to be this great fighter, but what happens if you lose? What happens if you don't meet your perfect standard for yourself? Where will your meaning be then, Owen? You want logotherapy, Owen? Here it is. What will your life be after fighting?"

"Fuck off. I'm out of here. This is my last time seeing you, Dr. Greene. It's been a real fucking pleasure. Peace the fuck out."

13

"You should go back."

"Are you serious, Doc?? There's no way in hell I'm letting her talk to me again before my fight."

"There's a reason I chose her to be my replacement for you."

"Oh yeah? You took your stick that was up your ass and shoved up hers? Well hey Doc, leave me out of y'all's foreplay."

"Do you want to know the reason or not?"

"No, I don't want to know, but Jesus Christ, tell me anyway."

"She's a fighter too."

"Ha! Get fucked, Doc. She's a fighter??"

"I bet a Benjamin that she hasn't given up on you yet."

"A Benjamin?? Who the hell talks like that still? You're an old man. You shouldn't say words like Benjamin, Doc. And I don't have a hundred dollars to piss away right now."

"She's been through some shit, and she's come out the other side as a fighter. She never gives up on her patients. That's not her style. Dr. Greene is not this toxic feminine that you think she is—that's just you and your issues with women. I knew you'd pounce on her at some point, but I picked her because I knew she'd get up after being knocked down by you. She's probably tougher than you are. And she's definitely smarter . . . You need to go back."

"You're actually an asshole, you know that, Doc? You're an asshole.

"She's messing with my head, Doc.

"What if I start doubting myself? What if I get knocked out? She's not a sports psychologist. It's my brain cells I am gambling with here, Doc."

"You don't need a sports psychologist, Owen, you need someone like her."

"Well, we'll see. I've been feeling great lately. I've flipped a switch, and the chaos has calmed. Or maybe it's just focused in a direction now."

"Your issues aren't surface level stuff man; they lay deep in that maze of yours."

"My maze?"

"Your psyche."

"Hmmm . . . Do you want another beer?"

"Sure."

"Sweet, this round is on you. I'm out too. Oh, and hey, grab a vodka soda for Kelley. She should be here soon. Thanks, Doc!"

"Yeah, yeah, just make sure you get the next round."

"You look so skinny."

"Well, hello to you, Miss Sag Queen."

"You're an asshole for purposely leaving out the beautiful part."

"You started it. And I am getting ready for my fight."

"You have to be this skinny to fight someone?"

"I actually have 11 more pounds to lose . . . but I have three months to do it."

"You'll be a skeleton by then. The wind will blow you away. I'll give you a hug and break your spine. Am I going to have to be on top from now on? I hate being on top."

"You need your own show. You're a one woman act. Really though, I think they have an open mic here tonight. You should tell your little jokes."

"This dive bar wouldn't appreciate my talent or intellect. Where's Jon? I thought you said he was here with you?"

"Who's Jon?"

"Your friend."

"I don't have a friend here with me named Jon?"

"Yes, you do."

"No, I don't?"

"Then who are you here with?"

"I'm here with Doc."

"Are you fucking with me?"

"I feel like you're the one whose fucking with me."

"Wow . . . You're like, a real idiot."

"You know, you're coming in hot tonight. Could you ease up a little bit on the zingers?"

"Doc is Jon."

"Doc is Doc . . ."

"You're the only one that calls him 'Doc.'"

"There's no way that's true."

"Oh, here he is! Hey, Jon! How're you? Oh! For me? Vodka soda?? Thank you, Jon."

"You're still hanging around this guy?"

"YOUR NAME IS JON??"

"Why are you yelling at me?"

"Why'd you tell me that your name was 'Doc?'"

"I didn't."

" . . . Really?"

"Really."

"Well shit . . . this alters my whole perception of my reality. This is a crack in the lens that I see the world through . . ."

"I'm sure you'll survive somehow."

"I think I'll need another beer . . . Doc—I mean Jon, will you buy me another beer?"

"I bought the last one. You owe me about 18 drinks."

"You're counting?"

"Yep."

"You're a psycho for that . . . Doc thinks I need to go back to therapy. What do you think, Kelley?"

"You need to go back."

"Just like that? No hesitation? You aren't even going to ask me how I am doing?"

"You need to go back."

"Unbelievable. My feelings about my own psyche don't matter to you two?"

"No."

"You aren't to be trusted."

"This betrayal is unexpected . . . I was hoping for some support from you guys, but clearly that's too much to ask for . . . Doc thinks I need a female therapist."

"You do."

"We made love, Kelley! And this is how you treat me after??"

"I'm just being honest. You like honesty, don't you, Owen?"

"Was it that disappointing? I know it didn't last that long . . . But I gave a full effort into the prep! That has to count for something!"

"We are just trying to help you."

"Wait . . . are you two sleeping together? Is this why you're ganging up on me?? Is this why you won't buy me anymore drinks, Doc?!"

"He was voted 'Most Dramatic' in high school."

"I really was . . ."

"You're really going to fight a man in a cage in three months?"

"Sure am."

"Yeah, I still don't see it."

"You're as bad as Dr. Greene!"

"Where's it at?"

"It's in Portland."

"We'll come watch."

"Really?? Hell yeah. I love it when people in the audience actually care if I get hurt or not. It has to build up the suspense in y'all! Just for a beautiful climax. Winning an exciting fight is the perfect story."

"You're worried about us being nervous before you fight? Shouldn't you be worried about your own nerves?"

"Oh, I'll be fine. I just want everyone there to enjoy the show."

"Well, we'll be in the front row then. I'm sure we will get showered in your blood."

"Well . . . hopefully that won't happen . . . Wait! Are you into blood-play, Kelley? I don't think that's one of my kinks . . .

"Kelley wants to be a comedian, Doc."

"Comedy is a noble pursuit."

"Noble? Really?"

"Truths can be revealed under the veil of comedy that could never get discussed otherwise."

"He's right. Good comedy has philosophy in it."

"Comedy has a way of reflecting society back onto itself that we don't usually see."

"You use comedy in your writing, Owen."

"The voices in my head are just naturally funny sometimes."

"Laughter is impulsive—that's what makes it beautiful. A good joke can reveal a sliver of a 'through-line' that lives in most of our souls. The common impulse that we all share is that a certain joke is funny, and it's out of our control. It just happens, and the majority agrees. Or they don't, and the joke bombs. Then there is a subconscious agreement that that joke doesn't touch on the majority 'through-line' in the souls of the people listening to the joke."

"I didn't know you were such a fan of comedy, Jon."

"Can you call him 'Doc?' He doesn't seem like a 'Jon' to me yet."

"Comedy is fascinating to look at through the lens of a psychologist. I think we appreciate it more. Comedians are society's 'canaries in the coal mine.' They sound the alarm publicly first, and let us know when our systems are failing us. And through comedy, people listen, but more importantly, they really hear the message. You can't hold a mirror up to society and expect them to love you for it. Hell, we killed Socrates just for asking questions. We arrested Galileo for doing science . . . If you take a 'head on' approach to changing the world, the world will take your head for it. Many people will despise you for showing them how ugly we are, and where we need to change. But if it's done through comedy, if you almost 'trick' us into seeing our own reflection, then we are so much more likely to change our salience landscape. This is one of the reasons why 'The Trickster' is a part of so much mythology, and one of our archetypes we revert back to. 'The Trickster' embraces the chaos and pokes holes in our 'Order' we try to apply to the chaos."

"The comedian is 'The Trickster' in modern terms?"

"Yeah, in a way. The comedian is one of the many 'Tricksters.' A lot of artists draw from the chaos. Owen does it in his fighting and writing. "

"But Doc, do you know why the caged bird sings? It's out of fear, isn't it? Fear and hatred of her cage. We can fall in love with the songs about our cage. That's what my girl Maya said, anyway. I need another beer. You want one, Doc? Kelley? I'll be right back."

"He means Maya Angelou . . . The homeless are also 'canaries in the coal mine.' The more society fails us, the more homeless pop up. It's more of a direct and visual warning, rather than an artistic or comedic one."

"It's more than that though, isn't it, Jon? The homeless situation has many layers to it. It's not so black and white."

"Sure, nothing is black and white, but society is failing them. WE are failing them—you and me, and that is one of the big variables that contributes to the homeless crisis."

"Is it a crisis?"

"Look around . . . It's a crisis alright."

"But is it really up to us to fix all the problems in society?"

"If not us, then who else?"

"How about our elected officials?"

"You aren't serious, are you, Kelley? Is she serious, Doc? Here ya go."

"She's young."

"Sure, compared to you she is. Our elected officials don't do shit anymore, Kelley. They only serve their own self interest, which is making them money. They stopped serving us a long time ago. There's an argument to be made that comedians have more of an influence on the culture than politicians do."

"Are you going to make another one of your famous 'straw-man' arguments Owen? And what even is culture?"

"Do I really need to? I feel like most of us see this."

"'Most of us' is an optimistic perspective. I'd say the minority see the real problems in the West. Not the majority. We are too 'in it' to see it objectively."

"Is this how y'all's therapy sessions would go? Just talking in circles about society and the meaning of life?"

"Pretty much."

"So you guys never stopped?"

"Shit . . . I guess not."

"I am working on developing dialectic with people I respect. But I couldn't find anyone I respect, so I settled on Doc here. I'm attempting to come from the place of Philia Sophia."

"What's Philia Sophia?"

"It's something like, 'learning as a community for the love of wisdom.'"

"Oh."

"As opposed to Philia Nikkia, which is something like, 'the desire to learn from a place of wanting to be correct or right.'"

"One's the teacher and the other is the politician?"

"Some teachers teach from a place called Philia Nikkia though."

"And some therapists practice from that place too—like Dr. Greene."

"You're wrong, Owen. That's not her at all."

"You sure about that, Doc?"

"Yes, I am. You need to go back."

"Well, fuck, I guess I'll go back . . ."

"Remember your own motivation next time. The Philia Sophia. Come to her with the same energy you show up at my house with."

"You showed up at his house?"

"It was breakfast!"

"Uninvited?"

"IT WAS BREAKFAST!"

14

"How'd you know you wanted to be a fighter?"

"I never know how to answer questions like that, Kelley. Where do any of our dreams come from? I watched the movie *Rocky* a lot as a kid, and I was always mesmerized by the fights I saw on T.V. Something pulled me towards martial arts."

"Yeah, but what was it that pulled you?"

"I don't know."

"That's not that helpful."

"Sorry. That's just the way it is for me. Why are you asking anyway?"

"How about writing? How did you know that you wanted to do that?"

"That was something I always felt pulled towards too, but I put it on the back burner to make room for The Fighter to grow. I remember being 16 years old and telling people I'd be a writer. It wasn't until a bad breakup, the consumption of lots of sad music and wine, and a year of writing shitty poetry, before I realized I stumbled upon my dream again. I wrote because I HAD to. I was overwhelmed with emotion and I needed an outlet.

I was injured, so I couldn't train. I found writing and writing found me. Just like martial arts did 12 years ago."

"Can you hand me my underwear?"

"Sure, but I'm going to take it off you again in about 15 minutes. If that's alright with you?"

"Hmmm, we'll see about that."

"What's on your mind, Kelley?"

"I haven't felt *pulled* towards something in a very long time . . .

"I wanted to be a ballerina when I was nine."

"I wanted to be a NFL quarterback. Why a ballerina?"

"They're poetry in motion. They express so much emotion with just the movements of their bodies. Those ladies can tell whole stories. 'Mesmerizing.' That's what you said about martial arts . . . that's how I felt about dance."

"Art will do that to us."

"Yeah . . . I was pulled towards that. My mom even managed to get me into a dance class. She had to work an extra day a week to do it, and I pretty much begged her until she caved in . . . I went to that class for three years before we had to move again. He found us again . . ."

"Your dad?"

"Yeah . . . him."

"You never went to another class?"

"Nope. Then I grew. No human being has ever wanted to remain short more than I did when I was 12. But I grew seven inches in two years. I was long and lanky. Then my boobs came in and I knew I could never be a real ballerina. I was 15 when I realized that . . . Nothing has ever *pulled* me since then.

"And you know what??"

"What's that?"

"I was a horrible dancer! Why would God, or the Universe, or whatever, give a little girl such stupid big dreams, just to watch me give up on them? Why?"

"I don't know, Kelley . . ."

"I have to tell you something . . ."

"You have a twin sister?"

"No, I don't. You asshole. This is serious. Can you be serious for a second?"

"Hold on, let me check my programming. See, if you just hit this button right here you get 'super cereal mode activated,' but be careful when you push my buttons, I'm freakishly ticklish."

"Don't laugh at me . . . promise me you won't??!"

"Oh my God, Kelley, I solemnly swear I probably won't laugh at whatever you're going to tell me."

"Errr . . ."

"C'mon, it'll be okay."

"Well . . . You know how you and Jon were talking about comedy the other night?"

"Who's Jon?"

"Stop! Be serious!"

"I am being serious . . ."

"We were talking about comedy and the trickster. Do you remember?"

"Vaguely. I think I was cross-faded."

"Well . . . I felt pulled again."

"Pulled towards what?"

"Towards comedy."

"What about comedy?"

"I want to do it."

"Really??"

"Yeah, I mean, I've been thinking about it for the last few days, and I want to try it. I'm going to do an open-mic at our bar . . . I have a few jokes written already."

"Do you need help? You can practice in front of me, or we can figure out jokes together! Oh man, this is going to be fun!"

"Wait . . . you don't think it's a dumb idea?"

"Your new dream? It's a dream! You're being *pulled* again! It's fucking fantastic, kid!"

"You really think I can do it?"

"Of course you can! The idea has already grabbed you—it's already done! You just have to step back and let it come out of you now. The creative part is my favorite. But with comedy, you're the writer and the performer. That's two different kinds of creativity. It's so much more fun than what I do! Fucking bad-ass, Kelley."

"Wow . . . you aren't really an asshole are you?"

"Can I put on a podcast with a professor of psychology from the University of Toronto and a stand-up comedian?"

"Sure."

"Sweet!"

"Hey . . . will you take off my underwear and kiss me instead?"

"Oh yeah? Let me ask the little fella. Ohh, look at that, we got movement down there."

"Oh my god, shut up, you're going to ruin it. Go back to being relentlessly supportive."

"You want the dirty talk, huh? I got you. You're an incredible human, Kelley. And you're going to crush it as a comedian."

"Oh my . . . go on . . . kiss up my thigh too . . . Don't stop . . ."

"You.

"Have.

"A.

"Dream.

"Again.

"Lets run with it, Doll. Let's chase it. Let's see what we can do."

"Fuuuuuck, Owen. Come up here and fuck me."

"Yes ma'am."

15

"Owen?"

"Yes, Doll?"

"Why do you sing sad songs in bed after sex?"

"Huh? Are they sad? I guess I didn't notice."

"I like it. I'm not complaining. You have a nice voice sometimes. I like when you sing Johnny Cash."

"Oh yeah, you sing too! Will you sing me something?"

"Oh . . . I don't know . . ."

"If you don't want to, I completely understand."

"No . . . it's not that . . . Okay, I'll sing one song . . ."

" . . . Holy shit, Kelley! That was amazing! I had no idea! You never sing in the car or in the shower. Why not? It's beautiful!"

"Singing is deeply personal to me."

"Oh . . . well, I love it. Thank you for sharing with me."

"Owen?"

"Yeah?"

"I know you aren't fully here. Not all of you anyway."

"What do you mean? I'm right here."

"No . . . you aren't. But it's okay—it really is. I've noticed from the first time we met. You're keeping a part of yourself guarded. I think it belongs to someone else . . . I didn't think we'd end up hanging out again, so I didn't think it mattered . . . It doesn't matter, but, just so you know, I see it. I see that you're missing pieces."

"I'm sorry. I don't know what to say."

"We can still fuck. It's okay. I don't need all of you here; I'll take the pieces you're willing to give."

"Shit Kelley, it's not supposed to be like this . . ."

"I read your poetry."

"No! Kelley! You promised me you wouldn't!"

"I know . . . I just had to know who She is."

"Who?"

"Your other half. Your missing piece. I had to know why She has a spell on you . . . and why I don't . . . I had to meet Her."

"Kelley . . . I—"

"—It's okay! It really is. I understand you so much better now. Your writing was so sad Owen . . . so sad . . . and deep. I had no idea . . . I'm sorry She doesn't love you."

"No, Kelley, I am the one who is sorry."

"You deserve to be loved, Owen."

"Yeah, Kelley, but the thing is, so do you . . ."

16

"Well, hello, Owen. I wasn't so sure I'd see you again. I thought you had given up on me."

"Hey, Dr. Greene. I'd like to apologize for the last time I saw you, and for all of the times before that too . . . I haven't trusted you. Today I want to start."

"I'm thrilled to hear that, but what brought about this sudden change of attitude?"

"Doc helped . . . but also, I've been meaning to practice coming to people from a place of love. I want to practice having a dialectic from the place of Philia Sophia."

"You know Greek??"

"No, I just like philosophy."

"I think this is a good start."

"I get sucked into Philia Nikkia sometimes . . . I'm competitive, but I want to be competitive at the right time and place. Focusing it into something, like my fight, helps me be able to zoom out and see it from a different view. That's where I want to keep my competitive spirit. I want to leave it locked in that cage with me."

"Hmmm . . . This is good stuff you're realizing, Owen. and I completely agree with you but . . .—"

"—But what?"

"It won't be easy containing your competitiveness. It'll take a lot of work and self control. It'll be a lifelong process . . . and being able to balance being an athlete with the rest of your life . . . balancing the violence and the love . . . that's the trick, isn't it?"

"I can do it."

"Yeah, I feel like you can, Owen. Maybe not perfectly, but no one is perfect. You can tiptoe the lines between order and chaos, if you're willing to try."

"I am."

"How's training going?"

"I feel great. I'm sore, but the lungs are coming back and I am feeling strong. My striking has always been crisp, but it's the grappling that is giving me confidence. I used to hate it. I used to skip it. I used to suffer through it. For so long I did . . . Then, somewhere along the line, through the suffering, I got a little better. And now, looking back, I've come so far. That is something I will always be proud of."

"You took a weakness and made it a strength?"

"Exactly. I took my lead and turned it into gold."

"Alchemy?"

"You know about alchemy, Dr. Greene?"

"I was fascinated by it in my early twenties. And then there was Carl Yung . . . and that book."

"I have an unfinished book called, *The Alchemist Assistant.* I'm not super attached to the title.

"How come you haven't finished yet?"

"I think that's because I haven't lived it yet."

"Hmmm."

"I stopped drinking for the fight. Two months out and I cut alcohol and weed."

"You did? Just like that?"

"Yep."

"Any withdrawals?"

"I feel fantastic."

"Wow . . . I thought you were an addict?"

"I am. But not when I have a fight."

"That doesn't make logical sense, Owen. Addiction doesn't work like that."

"Says who?"

"The studies say so. And so much research."

"Well, Dr. Greene, I do this every time, and every time it's been easy to drop alcohol and weed."

"But why's it easy?"

"Because I want to win this fight in two months, way more than I want to get high today, or get drunk."

"Fascinating . . ."

"That's my meaning, isn't it? logotherapy?"

"Yeah . . . your artistic expression as a martial artist has a deep meaning to you.

"The fact that you're easily willing to sacrifice some of your vices for art is beautiful in its own way . . . Hearing you talk about it with such passion and perspective, I'm starting to feel different about it. I think it is healthy for you. At first, I wasn't sure, but now, I think you have good intentions, and not so much 'The will to power.'"

"Friedrich?"

"... You call Nietzsche, 'Friedrich?'"

"Well, that was his name. I call all the old-timers by their first names. Or I give them nicknames. I'm not calling that guy, *The Antichrist,* that's for sure."

"You're so strange sometimes."

"Thank you, Dr. Greene."

"He did have interesting ideas about art and meaning, didn't he?"

"Friedrich? Sure, I suppose you can say that. The death of God . . . Truth . . . He tried to warn us, Dr. Greene."

"Reminds me of you."

"What?! What about me reminds you of him?"

"Living for your art. Attempting to be great at something. And trying to figure out the truth without God."

"Hmmmm. I don't know about that."

"You disagree, Owen?"

"Friedrich was brilliant, but he was missing one of the key variables that contributes to meaning."

"What's that?"

"Other people. Our meaning lies in them too. It lives in our relationships. Fred had nasty views about women, didn't he? . . . I don't want to be like him in that way . . . Art AND other people, Dr. Greene. As far as I can tell, that's it."

"But, Owen . . . how many healthy relationships do you have?"

"I know . . . and my art isn't great either. That's why I am here, Dr. Greene. To work on my relationships. I need other people with the art. I can't just live for art alone. It's too lonely. I–uhh . . ."

"Yes, Owen?"

"Love. That's why I started coming to therapy. Learning how to be in love."

"You came to therapy to 'learn how to be in love?'"

". . . Yeah."

"Owen . . . Only the people we love can truly help us navigate through being in love with them."

"Have you ever been in love, Dr. Greene?"

"Well—"

"—I'm sorry, that's personal. I won't push for personal stories anymore. Sorry."

"No, no. It's alright. I've been in love twice. Once when I was 17 and another time when I was 24."

"You aren't married though, are you, Dr. Greene?"

"I was engaged for 6 years . . . He wanted to travel and party, and I wanted my career."

"I'm sorry, Dr. Greene."

"We got a dog together to see if we were going to want kids after the marriage. He ended up hating her. He started to call her mine and refused to help . . . I'm grateful we never got married . . . or had kids."

"Do you regret having been in love with them?"

"I don't regret Chad. I learned a lot about myself during that relationship that I would never have been able to see if it wasn't for his eyes reflecting my soul back to me in a weird way. "

"Chad was your fella you were engaged too?"

"Yeah. We haven't talked in years."

"How about when you were 17? Do you regret him?"

"Tony was my first love . . . I was so young . . . Just a girl. I knew nothing about the real world . . . He played baseball and lived on a ranch. Tony was more old school than most men I've ever known . . . I regret loving him."

"Dr. Greene, what happened?"

"Remember my senior year? My high school teacher?"

"Ohh, yeah . . ."

"Well, Tony didn't believe me . . . I came to him first . . . He said that I must've asked for it . . . He said . . . I was a whore . . . He said that I cheated on him. The whole community said I was a whore who was trying to ruin the career of a fine young teacher . . . The narrative around town was that I was the whiny drama queen who was messing with the head of the state's best short-stop. They were more worried about a State Championship than me . . . My family fought it. They believed me. But we couldn't afford a good lawyer . . . I met my best friend, Caitlin, at Berkeley. She came from a family of lawyers and she loved to argue and drink. She was the only one during that time that really listened to me . . . Anyway . . . Owen?"

"Yes?"

"That's enough about me."

"Yes, ma'am. I know it doesn't make any difference, or alleviate the suffering you've gone through . . . but I am sorry that happened to you."

"It's okay. It lit a fire under my ass and now I am one of the top psychologists in the state. Tony is still on his ranch and Chad is the principal of a high school. Our lives merged for a few years and then diverged. That's life though, isn't it, Owen? People come and go, but it's up to us to remain steady and true to ourselves. We have to be grounded with who we are or the tides of life will sweep us away."

"So, no one knows how to love?"

"I think you are asking the wrong question, Owen. Trying to be in love is like trying to grab a fistful of water; the tighter you squeeze, the more the love squirts out through the cracks in our fingers. Like life, we must flow with love. Never damning it or swimming against the current. I just want you to know that I believe therapy needs to be more human engagement, rather than science. I think you feel the same way, am I right?"

"Dr. Greene?"

"Yes, Owen?"

"I'm in love with someone who doesn't give a shit about me . . ."

"I know, Owen, I know . . ."

"Some days, it hurts so much . . . I've just been . . . waiting. Waiting for the day she loves me back . . . I think I tried to become a man she could love . . . That's why I started to write. She's why I read so much . . . She's why I love poetry . . . Every cheesy love song reminds me of her . . . Every time I hear an ambulance, I pray to a God—that I am not sure is real—that it's not her in the screaming van . . . I learned the guitar . . . So I could play for her some day . . . I haven't spoken to her in a year now. My soul aches, Dr. Greene."

"I'm sorry, Owen. We all want to be loved by someone. Intimately sharing our individual experience with someone else is beautiful. I know why you ache for it. You have to keep trying, Owen."

"Dr. Greene?"

"Yes, Owen?"

"Remember Kelley? We talked about her?"

"I'm going to help her write jokes."

"Oh really? Jokes? What for?"

"She's going to do stand-up."

"Oh! Wow. How interesting! Stand-up comedy is uniquely—"

"—Dr. Greene?

"I think she loves me."

"Oh?"

"I don't love her . . . She's going through the same thing I am . . . She says it's okay though. She says she doesn't need me to love her fully. She says she is okay . . . but she isn't, is she? She isn't okay . . . I know it because . . . I am not okay."

17

"Is he sleeping?"

"No, I'm not sleeping. I'm dying."

"Only two more hours until we're there. Drink your spit and stop bitchin."

"Five hours until weigh-in though.

"We should stop soon to stretch and move around."

"Sure thing. You hungry, Kelley?"

"I'm starving actually—"

"—Hey! No food talk, please. Use sign language or pig latin or something. I'm a literal skeleton back here, guys. I'm not strong enough to listen to you two talk about KFC right now. I'll cave guys. I'll drink water! The gravy guys! The gravy!"

". . . Is he delirious?"

"It's entirely possible. He's extremely dehydrated. He'll be fine though. Don't worry, Kelley, this is normal for a fighter. KFC sounds good to me. Is it okay with you, Kelley?"

"Screw you, Doc."

"KFC sounds great!

"So how do you know so much about fighting, Jon?"

"Doc wrestled in college. He was pretty good too."

"Is that true?"

"Yeah."

"Wrestling is worse. You have to stay on weight all season. I just have to stop drinking and diet a little for a few weeks."

"Yeah, but then you drop eight pounds of water weight in two days."

"Well, yeah."

"You are skinny."

"I'll be up 10-15 pounds tomorrow for the fight. The fight is so much easier than the weight cut."

"Are you delirious?"

"I don't think so . . ."

"I'm not so sure he'd be able to tell if he was."

"He has a point. I'm glad I have you two Samwise Gamgee's to carry me up the mountain."

"What's he talking about?"

"You're more like Gandalf 'The Gray', Doc. Sorry, you aren't Gandalf 'The White' yet. Maybe someday you'll transform like the caterpillar into the beautiful butterfly white wizard guy. But right now, like this, you're still a gray caterpillar Hufflepuff thingy."

"Should we listen to music?"

"Wait! No! I want to talk to you guys! God my mouth is so dry. Can I get, like, two drops of water?"

"What did you last weigh?"

"136.3"

"How long ago?"

"Two hours ago."

"Just two drops. Watch him, Kelley! Make sure only two drops."

"Sheesh, this is intense."

"I think that was four drops."

"Kelley! You rat!"

"You're cutting it close man."

"I know, I know. I'll be fine. I'll do jumping jacks while you guys are in KFC. No way can you bring that gravy in the car with me. And I'd appreciate it if you two washed your hands after—with the soap in the bathroom and with their wet wipes. Get all the chicken smell off yourselves."

"See? Now he is talking like his usual annoying self. He'll be fine."

"No, Jon, I don't think he will be fine."

"What? Why's that?"

"Kelley, I—"

"—Did you hear him call me a rat?"

"Is that not a term of endearment he uses for you?"

"Kelley, I'm near death! I—"

"—You aren't fighting some guy with a face tattoo and big muscles, pal—you're fighting me!"

"'Pal?' Shit! I'm sorry! I'm sorry! I'm sorry! I didn't mean like a literal rat. I—"

"—I know what you meant asshole. It doesn't change shit."

"I'm sorry, Doc, she has such a dirty mouth. I—"

"—Now is not the time for your wise guy routine, Bucko."

"First pal? Now Bucko? You're really emasculating me right before I have to go fight—"

"—Don't call me a rat. It's pretty simple."

"Yes, ma'am, understood."

"How old are you two?"

"Hey, Doc, our generation is growing up slower than yours did. It's not good to compare generations anyway, so don't get carried away judging us. I'm a young 30, you know what I'm trying to say, Doc?"

"You say it so proudly, though."

"I know what he's trying to say, Owen."

"Yeah . . . I know too . . . Owen 'Peter Pan' Day. Should I change my fighter nickname to that? Doesn't really strike fear in the hearts of my competition, though."

"What's your current fighter nickname?"

"The Alchemist."

"That's kind of bad-ass."

"I know."

"I'm walking out to Phil Collins too."

"In *The Air Tonight*?"

"Yep."

"Bad-ass."

"I know. I'm stoked."

"Are you nervous at all?"

"I'm thirsty. And hungry. That's the thing about weight cuts, they suck so bad that you almost forget you're even fighting soon. There's almost no time to get nervous."

"Do you ever get nervous?"

"I didn't in my last fight."

"Not at all? Not even for a second?"

"Not at all."

"This was three years ago?"

"Yep. Three years ago."

"It's been three years since you fought?"

"Yep."

"Are you worried about ring rust?"

"How about we stop talking about the fight for a while. Are you dating anyone, Doc? Did you get on the apps yet?"

"What's ring rust?"

"Ring rust is when a fighter isn't as sharp because he hasn't competed in a long time."

"Oh. Yeah, are you worried about that??"

"I'm not."

"Well, that's good, I guess. I think I am getting pretty nervous for you."

"They say nervousness and excitement are very similar, and almost exchangeable. Just add in a little different perspective, trick the brain, and it's possible to understand your nerves as excitement. And what is excitement but a form of joy?"

"It's not that easy, Peter Pan."

"Which part isn't easy, Dr. Pepper?"

"Tricking the brain."

"How so?'

"The brain tricking the brain? How?"

"Well, what about placebo stuff?"

"That's someone else tricking you. Don't get me wrong, self-deception is one of our best and strongest adaptive responses, but it's hard to consciously trick our own brain; probably impossible. It has to come from the subconscious mind, not the conscious one."

"Sometimes I forget he was a psychologist, Kelley."

"I'm a professor of psychology now."

"You got the job?"

"Congrats, Jon!!"

"I start in the fall. It's a ways away, but it'll give me plenty of time to prepare."

"Breakfast paid off then?"

"You broke into my house?"

"And you got a job out of it! Sounds like it paid off to me!"

"Are you excited, Jon?"

"I am."

"You seem thrilled."

"I really am excited."

"What's it pay?"

"Not great."

"Well, that's a bummer."

"It's okay. Money isn't everything. I think I'll enjoy being a teacher."

"He says that now, but when I am rich and he needs a couch to sleep on, we'll see what's what then."

"What will be what?"

"I mean he can still sleep on the couch, I'm just going to make him feel really bad about using up all of my toilet paper."

"I think it's great, Jon."

"I do too. Seriously. You've been a great student of mine, Doc, and I think you are finally ready to take on some students of your own. Fly away little bird. I've taught you enough. Spread your wings and take to the sky."

"Thank you, Kelley. And Owen, thank you for believing in me while I was at a low point."

"Aw, don't sweat it, Doc! You'd do the same for me. So, Kelley, I probably should've mentioned this before . . ."

"What?"

"My father will be there."

"Oh?"

"Yeah . . . and I'll be a little busy."

"Yeah, you will be."

"So you're going to have to hang out with him."

"This is how I am meeting your father?"

"Well . . . yes?"

"Okay."

"Okay?"

"Yeah, okay. That's fine. You haven't said a lot about him yet, only that he likes sports and collecting things."

"Yep, that's him."

"Well, what else is there?"

"I'm sure there's more . . . He likes fishing, hunting, golfing, beautiful women, and Modest Mouse."

"Hey, I like Modest Mouse, too!"

"Well, there you go. You guys can talk about me and how great I am, and Modest Mouse."

"That's all there is to your father? We never really got around to him in therapy."

"I remember he cried when my parents first told us they were getting divorced. Only time I've ever seen him cry, and he lost it. Completely lost it. It was heartbreaking . . .

"And he was very enthusiastic about competition. That's a really nice way of putting it . . . We spent a lot of hours practicing baseball, basketball, and football. He coached me in some of them. I think he thought I was going to be some sort of pro athlete. I think that was the dream he had for my brother and I . . . Didn't really work out that way though . . ."

"What're you talking about? You're making your father's dream for you come true tomorrow. You'll be a pro athlete when those cage doors get locked."

"Shit . . . You're right . . . Uhh, Doc?

"Yeah?"

"I thought this was MY dream for my life?"

18

"Hello, Owen, I—oh shit! Your face! Your fight?"

"If you think this is bad, you should see the other guy's hands."

"Are you alright? Are those stitches?"

"I'm fine, Dr. Greene. We definitely have a lot to talk about, but physically I'll be fine. The fight didn't go as bad as you're thinking for me. I lost a split decision . . . He was good. He ate a lot of shots and used his wrestling. My alchemy didn't hold up this time . . . He out grappled me . . . Nice guy though. Way sweeter than I was expecting to be, honestly. He thought I won and I thought he won. It was close. But holy shit, Dr. Greene, it was hard! I fought with everything I had. I was exhausted and beat to shit by the end of it . . . I was happy when it was over . . . The weight cut wasn't great, but that's just an excuse."

"I'm proud of you for stepping in there at all. Most people wouldn't have the guts to do what you do."

"Thank you, Dr. Greene, but it's just what I do. Some people paint, some people play the piano, and I fight. I do think I need to be humbled sometimes, though."

"Owen, you keep saying that. I think that's what makes you more humble than you think. Are you going to fight again?"

"I think so . . . I think I'll box, though, and not cut a lot of weight. I'm not going to think much about it for the next few weeks. Kelley is doing a bigger show in Portland this weekend. We're busy getting ready. She's doing amazing and we are having a blast writing together. She's really taken to philosophy. I think it's both an attempt to relate to me more, but also to improve our jokes."

"So are you two in a relationship now?"

"You know, we haven't really talked about it."

"But you care about her?"

"Yeah, I do."

"Not enough to be in a relationship with?"

"I don't know yet . . ."

"You have to purposely expose yourself to what you fear, Owen. Remember? I know your fear is getting hurt. Are you still not over Her?"

"I'll never be over Her, Dr. Greene. She changed me forever and I am forever changing because of Her."

"What is it about Her though? What's different about Kelley?"

"She brought out a side of me I wasn't aware was there. The Artist was only born because of Her. Being around Her is intoxicating. 'She's the poison I choose to sip on . . .' I used to say that a lot . . . She made me want to grow in every way imaginable. She made me want to understand Her. I want to listen to all of Her music, read all of Her books, eat all of Her food, and hear all of Her stories. I want to support Her in everything she does.

I haven't been able to stop daydreaming about Her since I met Her. It's only because of Her that I wanted to go from something like a boy to a man . . . But she never loved me. I never felt it back . . .

"That was okay with me though. She was going through a lot at that time . . . She lost someone she loved . . ."

"Do you romanticize Her by using Her as your muse?"

"100%, I do that."

"So, how are you sure all these feelings about Her are even real?"

"Oh, I know alright. I know."

"Hmmm. Okay, Owen, we'll come back to Her later. What about Kelley? Why do you care about her?"

"Kelley is like a sexy version of a younger me, before I met Her. I know that sounds narcissistic, but it doesn't feel like that when I am with her. She was just a little lost for a while . . . But seeing her get this excited about her comedy reminds me of when I first started to fight. I was so enthusiastic, motivated, and energetic. I put so much of myself into training. There's a certain energy that comes along with starting a new goal, and it's contagious. Kelley is smart and still wants to learn more. She is passionate and funny. We connect so effortlessly. We can talk about anything. I can roast her and she can roast me, and it's fun. And the sex is bananas. I think she is going to make it as a comedian. I really do."

"And she loves you?"

"Yeah . . . and that . . . I wish I loved her back, Dr. Greene . . . I wish it with everything in me! I wish I could just forget about

Her and move on . . . I've wished for that for a year now, but I can't forget it. The feelings for Her are haunting me."

"Owen, maybe you aren't here because 'you don't know how to be in love,' but because you're in love with the wrong person?"

"But, Dr. Greene, we don't get to choose who we love. In a sense, it's out of our control. It's something we just 'fall into,' isn't it?"

"Yes and no."

"Yes and no? How so?"

"We have some. We can control our attitudes."

"Do we? As far as I can tell, we don't control who we fall in love with, our dreams, our behavior, our laughter, our family, and the time and place we are born into. Dr. Greene, we don't have control over any of the important things that happen to us during our life. If we have free will, then it's just a millimeter in the infinite sea of chaos and order.

"I don't want to love the person that I do . . . And . . . My dreams aren't mine."

"What do you mean?"

"Being a professional athlete was my father's dream for me . . ."

"You realized this before the fight?"

"On the drive up. Doc pointed it out.

"It is obvious, Dr. Greene. I can't believe we never saw it before."

"Our ability to deceive ourselves is one of our strongest adaptive responses to consciousness."

"Yeah, I know. Doc said the same exact thing . . . That and this love shit have me fucked up, Dr. Greene."

"Must've been hard to come to terms with that realization before your fight."

"I almost didn't fight. Doc and Kelley pushed me to go through with it, and even though I lost, I'm glad I did it. I was nervous for the first time before a fight. I felt the fear deep in my bones . . . And I did it anyway . . . Somehow that is better than not having fear at all."

19

"Good evening, Portland, you filthy animals! I'm Kelley Jackson. How's everyone doing tonight?

"Alright, alright, alright.

"That's my impression of Matthew Mconaughey if he was a 28 year old single female without a plan for her future. But, hey! That's why I can be here telling jokes for all 25 of you homeless people tonight!

"This is for charity, right?

"Oh? You guys aren't homeless?

"It's hard to tell here in Portland. Everyone seems to be homeless. I heard someone say that it's just 'street camping.' Then he pulled down his pants and started to masturbate.

"But hey, that's just Portland, right?

"Keeping it weird, that's what y'all wanted?

"Well mission fucking successful, I'd say.

"Bravo guys, you've done it. Y'all are the weirdest white people on the planet.

"People from Portland look like they haven't seen the sun in four years . . .

"Oh? Y'all haven't?

"That makes sense.

"I think even the X-men would avoid Portland.

"They'd definitely have plenty of crime to fight though.

"And they'd blend in perfectly.

"I feel like Portland will become its own country someday and take over the rest of America.

"I'm serious folks! Remember when Seattle tried to do that? They did a pretty solid job too! They created their own world inside of ours, remember guys?? That shit was wild!

"And then . . . Well, then it started to get weird, didn't it? Anarchy is tricky, isn't it?

"But Portland is already weird! Y'all are more prepared than they were. You guys have been practicing for years. Y'all are Gay Day preppers. And good for you! Y'all are ahead of your time.

"But yeah, Portland will take over the world. San Francisco, Seattle, Portland, and L.A.—in 10 years I envision an alliance between those places, and then world domination.

"I mean think about it! That's where all of America's gays, queers, trans, and everything else in between live! And let's be honest here, they're better than the rest of us.

"I see some of you really don't like that one. The insecure straight males all stiffened up real quick!

"But stop and think about it!

"They have the best and worst qualities of the two genders.

"That's both exciting and terrifying, isn't it? Although, some people think blurring these lines is dangerous . . . I think they are just resistant to change.

"Let's be honest . . . there is no slowing things down, or getting off of the ride. All we can do is, try to nudge this ship towards an ideal.

"Remember the show *Survivor*?? A crazy social experiment, right? Viewed in front of millions and 'played' for a million dollars. It was like *Lord Of The Flies* but the Hollywood version. Actually, knowing Hollywood, they probably would've preferred to keep using kids . . . But anyway, that's a different joke. Who won the first season of *Survivor*? Who won it? A 6'2 hairy gay man!

"He walked around naked and played those other contestants brilliantly. Ruthlessly.

"He did!

"He was petty and cutthroat. He would spread rumors and lies. He was an expert manipulator. And he held his own in the physical challenges.

"You guys remember this, right??

"The LGBTQ community is better than the rest of us. It's a fact. Okay, maybe not a fact, but a theory I have.

"They are like all the hybrid cars everyone here drives.

"No! Think about it!

"They are the better combination of the masculine and the feminine, why wouldn't they be better? Richard from *Survivor* was better!

"So, yes, I think they'll take over the world. I think *Survivor* showed that to us. I think Seattle, Portland, San Francisco, and L.A. have shown us that.

"The future is gender-less!" That's what the homeless man yelled at me as he was climaxing.

"At least . . . I think he was homeless . . . maybe he wasn't? . . . It really is hard to tell here . . .

"Oh, no way! He's here! Right there! The masturbater!

"What do you do sir?

"A city councilman? Well . . . that makes sense. I—"

"—You aren't funny!"

"Oh look, another man telling a woman what she is. We've spotted the insecure straight one, guys! Don't you know that us feminists fought for our opportunity to be as toxically masculine as yo—"

"Get off the fucking stage! You're a bitch!"

"Uhhh . . . Security? Can we get this fuck-boy out of here? He's had one too many IPAs.

"Can't hold your booze, sir? It's okay, I'm sure he has a boyfriend in his tent he has to secretly see. See ya later, Mr. Councilman! Everyone say goodbye!"

"Fuck you, cunt!"

"Oh my! Cunt? I haven't heard a good 'cunt' in a long time!

"Well, I'm glad that's over with. Can we get back to the jokes?

"Don't worry folks, he isn't really a city councilman. And he wasn't the masturbater . . .

"That guy is probably breaking into your car right now, just to sit in the back seat, shoot up, and drop loads of semen everywhere. That's how they mark their territory around here, isn't it?

"You can see some of the richer white folks sweating now? Some of you guys really do want to check on your Teslas, huh?

"Oh, you guys are hilarious.

"I really do love Portland, though. I do. Portland has the most strip clubs per capita. This city supports so many struggling women by giving them job opportunities like stripping, sex work, or selling drugs. It's bloody brilliant! If I don't make it telling jokes, I know where I am moving.

"So, y'all will be cop-less, homeless, and gender-less soon? That's the plan, isn't it?

"That's like the triple crown of woke-ness!

"I'm rooting for you guys. I believe in you. But in all seriousness, maybe this is the future of western society . . .

"And maybe it is for the best . . .

"I know I've been hard on you guys tonight, but that's only because I see the potential here! Truly!

"You, and by you, I mean WE, have the opportunity to lead the way and set an example for the next generation. We can show them that a world that accepts everyone is possible some day. The streets of Portland might not be pretty right now, but that's because our job isn't done yet! In fact, it'll never end. It's a forever war . . . but it's worth fighting.

"So don't fuck it up!

"Be smart about it . . .

"And remember . . .

"It has to stop raining around here at some point.

"Well that's my ten minutes, guys! You've been great! Don't forget to follow me on social media, @ComedyKelley. I'll be back in Portland in a few months. Love y'all!"

20

"Kelley! Over here! Kelley!"

"She was so great, wasn't she, Doc? She delivered it perfectly! That asshole didn't phase her at all. She's tough, isn't she? Fuck yeah, Doc. Fuck yeah. She's incredible. Her potential is limitless, don't you think? It was only her third open mic and she killed it!"

"Hey! So? How'd I do?"

"You didn't hear us?? Oh my god, Kelley, you killed! It was fucking fantastic! You really couldn't hear us?? Everyone was laughing so hard, so I understand if you didn't! It was great! I am so proud of you."

"Well, I couldn't have done it without you."

"I bet you could've! You're a natural up there!"

"What do you think, Jon? How'd I do?"

"You crushed it, kid. You cut right to the core, made it relatable, spun it, and then left the crowd hopeful; maybe even inspired. It was a little idealistic for my taste, and I'm assuming that it was influenced by Mr. Romantic over here, but it was overall excellent. That was more than just jokes. I'm proud of you too. Let me buy you a drink."

"Thank you, Jon. I really appreciate it. I couldn't have done it without you, either. But about that drink—I'm beat. I don't think I'm up for it. Are you guys okay with heading back to the hotel?"

"Of course! Whatever you want to do. It's your night, Kelley."

"I'm just tired now that it's over. Let's go watch a movie or something in the room. Order food and champagne, just us three. Cool?"

"Let's do it."

"So, do you guys remember where we parked? I hate these streets."

"It's over here. Just take a lef—"

"—Hey cunt! Fuck you!!"

"Oh shit! It's that guy! He's got a gun! Kelley loo–

"Kelley!!!

"No! No! No! No!

"It's alright! It's alright!

"Doc! She'll be alright?! Doc? Kelley! Look at me! You'll be fine! You will be! Just believe it, okay? Believe you'll be okay! Doc?! Stop the bleeding! Doc! I'm begging you! Kell—"

"—Owen . . ."

"Shhhh, Kelley, don't speak! Don—"

"—don't tell me to 'shhh' . . . you asshole . . .

"I love you . . . You asshole . . . I . . . love you . . . Don't let me die, Owen . . . I don't want to yet. Don't . . . let me go . . . Please?"

"I won't! I won't! Kelley! Believe! You'll be okay! Say it with me!

"Kelley!"

"I wanted to be a canary . . . was I . . . ?

" . . . It sounded so . . . beautiful . . .

So . . ."

"Kelley!! Don't close your eyes! Don't do it! Look at me! Believe! Please! The power of belief! It'll work! Miracles can happen!

"Doc! Pray! Doc! Pray to your God!!

"You were beautiful, Kelley! You'll do it again at your next show! You just have to believe, Kelley! Believe you'll be okay and don't you fucking close your eyes!"

"It sounded so . . .

"Meaningful . . .

. . .

. . ."

"No! Kelley!!

"No! Believe! It's not over yet!

"You have so much life left! Doc!! Help me! Wake her up! She's not gone! Not yet! There has to be some life left! Doc! Doc! Doc! Doc . . .

"Doc!!

"Kelley!! Don't go! Kelley! You're a beautiful soul! Your life is so meaningful to me! You can't go! I need you! Kelley!

. . .

. . .

. . ."

"Let me in, Owen. I have breakfast."

"Respectfully, Doc, fuck off. Don't come back here. Leave me alone."

"Sure, Owen. Whatever you want."

"Go away, Doc. Not today."

"I don't have anything to say to you, Doc. Go away. Stay away. Fuck off. Tell Sara to piss off, too. I don't need your help. I can't handle anyone else. I can't handle anything else . . . Just let me be. Seriously. I'm not fucking around here, Jon."

"Okay."

"Hey Doc. Go away Doc, but leave the food. Oh, leave the booze, too. Thanks."

"Bye, Owen. Drink some water and take a walk."

"I'm still staring at my walls, Doc . . . Not yet . . . I have nothing to say. I can't hear anything. I can't feel anything more than this . . . I don't have the capacity. My cup is full . . . or empty . . . maybe empty? . . . No . . . full! I am too drunk and full of grief. I can't take anything else . . . I can't handle it . . . I keep waiting for someone to tell me that it wasn't real. That she is still here. That it was a dream. I keep waiting for reality to go back to what it was . . . but . . . it won't. There is no going back. It is what it is . . . I can't swallow it though. I can't let it be real. I can't talk to you, Doc. I can't talk to anyone. I can't talk about it . . . So fuck off, will ya?"

"You, just as you are. I don't need you to be anything else but that."

"I'm going to get pissed at you."

"That's okay."

". . . Doc?"

"Yes, Owen?

". . . Owen?"

"Why didn't your God save her?"

"I don't know, Owen. I don't know . . ."

"I can't eat today. You can take your food with you and go."
"Okay."

"... It is what it is ...
"I'll stay numb to it."

"So, Jon, why did your God let her die?"

"I don't know why."

"Why did he make the man that killed her?!"

"I don't know."

"Why'd he pump her up full of false dreams??

"Why, Jon?!! Why?!

"We did it, Jon! We spewed our bullshit, she soaked it up and it got her fucking killed! We killed her! We killed her! Get the fuck out of here!! I fucking hate you and your God! Neither one of you saved her! I couldn't save her! 12 years of fighting and I was powerless to do anything to stop that man . . .

"Get the fuck out!"

"Numb little bug. That's what I am now. A numb little bug . . .

"I wonder where Doc put my weed . . ."

"Hey, Bubba, have you seen the remote? I watched this episode yesterday, didn't I? It's time you got a job, dude. All you do is lay around and pee on things. I'm glad I have you to lay around with, though. You just have to start contributing to bills around here. We might go broke if you don't."

"God! Where the hell are you??

"It's not worth it! It's not!

"Take it all back! Please!!

"If this is the price for great art, then it isn't worth it!

"I shouldn't have to suffer in real life to write about it!

"Why'd she have to die? Answer me!

"Fuck you!

"I wanted to know Her perspective, so I had to lose someone too?

"No . . . Fuck . . . This isn't what I asked for!!

"Not like this . . .

"I prayed just one time that I'd gain a new perspective on what She was going through back then . . .

"But . . . not like this . . .

"I had to lose Her to get Her just to come to the understanding that I never even had Her? God? Are you even fucking there? Is this how you do business?! You kill people?!

"I asked for this . . . it's true. I invited Her into my house. Made it Our house, just to lose Her again, to remind me that

I never had Her in the first place . . . She never belonged to anyone . . .

"But God? I knew this. I knew it all already!!

". . . Why'd I have to live it too?

"It turns out . . . It really isn't that easy to change . . . Is that it, God? It isn't that easy to *know* something, is it?

"Where are you?!"

"'. . . In order to change, you have to rage against the order,
And fist-fight God,
And the devil,
Just to move your life . . .
. . . an inch.'"

"Is that right, God? That's what I wrote once, didn't I??

"I had to really believe it?

"I had to live it . . . To see the other side . . . and gain a new perspective.

"Even after all of this . . .

"I still know . . .

"It isn't enough . . .

"It isn't even close . . .

"There's no way to actually know what someone went through, is there God?

"No . . . their experience is uniquely their own? Isn't it?

"I'll never understand Her, will I?

"I never needed to . . .

"But honestly . . .

"I am glad I tried to.

"Hey, Bubba . . . I'm losing my God Damn mind.

"I'm talking to shadows on these walls . . ."

31

"Hello, Owen."

"Hello, Dr. Greene."

"A lot has happened since we last spoke."

"A lot has happened."

"And a lot of time has passed. How're you doing?"

"I'm okay."

"Are you really? You know, it's okay if you aren't?"

"I've managed to piece myself together."

"It's been nine months since Kelley passed . . . I haven't seen you in almost a year.

"Your haircut looks nice."

"Thanks, Dr. Greene. It's okay, you don't have to tease me. Enough with the foreplay. You can probe me. It's okay."

"Well . . . How're you? Really?"

"I'm surviving . . ."

"You once gave me words, 'not that it will ease your suffering or anything, but . . . ,' you said something like that to me once, do you remember?"

"I remember."

"I want you to know that I know there isn't anything I can say or do here that'll ease your suffering . . . but I wish I could.

"All I know is that she would want you to keep fighting. For fuck's sake, Owen, she'd want you to!

"She'd be screaming at you to get off your ass—your fight is just beginning!"

". . . Dr. Greene?"

"C'mon, Owen! You know she'd want you to pick yourself up and keep moving forward."

"Forward? Is that the way things move? I'm not so sure, Dr. Greene . . .

"Listen, Dr. Greene, I know you're saying things, but I can't really hear you."

"Get up off your ass and make your moves!"

"Moves? Like a game? I—I don't think this is therapy, Dr. Greene . . . "

"Where's The Fighter? Where's The Alchemist? Did they die too? Or do you just have more lead now?? Was it all bullshit??"

"Jesus, Dr. Greene . . ."

"She'd be disappointed in you.

"She'd be disgusted with how you've treated Jon.

"She'd hate you for it."

"Fuck off Sara! You didn't know her!"

"You're right. I didn't know her. Jon did talk to me about her. And how you were trying again with her. He thought she was great for you."

"What? You and Jon talk about me behind my back??"

"This whole case has been special . . .

". . . Jon broke a lot of laws for you, and look at how you repay him?

"He gave up his career for you.

"He risked everything . . . fuck's sake man, I'VE RISKED EVERYTHING!"

"Dr. Greene . . . I don't understand."

"Jon gave me a letter from Kelley. She asked him to give it to me. He refused to. He told her that she couldn't contact me. He said that it was what was best for you. She told him that she just had a few questions for me. She persisted and he took the letter just to appease her, but he had no intention of ever giving it to me. But after she passed, he decided to show me. I want to read it to you, if that's alright?"

"What? Er—Dr. Greene, I don't understand . . .

"I read our texts and look through our photos all the time . . . I can still hear her voice like she was right next to me. I call her phone to just hear her voicemail . . . I've been dying to hear her say something new to me . . . and . . . but she's gone . . . and... and this letter? I don't understand . . ."

"It's about you."

"Me? I, uh—Kelley, really? . . . I get to hear her voice again?"

"I'm going to go ahead now and read it. Is that okay, Owen?"

"Yeah . . . sure. Go ahead . . ."

"Hey, Sara—"

"—She called you Sara?"

"Can I continue, Owen?"

". . . Yeah."

"—Hey, Sara. I want to talk to you about Owen. And about myself. I wish I could see him with your eyes. I know Jon probably won't ever give this to you. But still, I needed to write this. So about Owen—he's doing good, for the most part. I see the moments when he stares off into the distance, in pain. His eyes reveal how his soul is aching. It's not a new look though. He's just been doing it a little more since he fought. I used to think before, when he'd stare out into the nothingness, that he was thinking about Her—probably recalling a memory, or writing a poem. But now, I know that his heart aches all the time, about so many different things. I think his bad posture has to do with carrying too much weight on his shoulders. Do you know what I'm trying to say? He's been hyper focused on me and my comedy, which I think is helping him cope with losing the fight —and with losing his dream. Seeing him go through this has me a little scared about going to Portland next week. I won't tell him that though. He needs me to be strong right now, right?

"Besides being scared, and knowing he loves someone else, I'm doing good. I'm happy most days. Owen and Jon have been so inspiring to me. You three are so driven to make a difference in the world, that I want to try too. I have to try. I've been floating around from thing to thing so meaninglessly for so long now. But recently, I've had direction, and it feels so good. This is what something like progress feels like, right? Growth?

"Owen has been asking a lot about what narcissism looks like in women lately, and Sara, I wasn't sure how to answer him at first. We talked it out and decided that on the surface it looks like manipulation, control, and an obsession about appearance; but it's so much deeper than that isn't it? He is so convinced that it's all envy. I wish I could ask you about it. I wish we could talk. I have so many questions for you. One being, as us women climb the ladder of power in America, how do we avoid inheriting the qualities we think are 'toxically masculine.' There's a brand of feminism currently that promotes sleeping with whomever we want, gaining power and status by any means necessary, and dominating men. What's that saying, 'Power corrupts and absolute power corrupts absolutely?' As women gain power, we are influenced by the power we gain, aren't we? Don't we have a greater responsibility to be mindful of our behavior than ever because we are so much more influential in society than ever before? Does that make any sense to you? I remember learning about Alice Paul and the women's suffrage movement, and I just feel like the women of the past would hate it if we naturally inherited the qualities in men that they fought so hard against. Have we come full circle? And has there been a spike in narcissism in women lately? Seems like there would be, but no one is talking about it.

"Owen's been trying hard lately to 'understand the feminine experience better.' It's cute and exhausting, but sometimes it's hard to explain it to him. I think he hears it, and really is trying, but can't quite understand. Maybe people who have identified as male their whole lives will never understand? I do like that he is trying though. He really has come a long way, and I know that's thanks to you and Jon. Being around those two makes me feel safe. Do you know what I'm talking about, Sara? I think I'll try to find a therapist of my own. Everything that Jon and Owen have said about you makes me wish you could be my therapist, but I understand, Owen needs you. Well, I'm off to work now. Looking forward to the weekend and the show! Wish me luck! And stay in touch! Ha, yeah, right."

"Owen?"

"Yeah?"

"Are you with me?"

"Uh-huh . . ."

"We all see what she saw in you."

". . . And what's that?"

"Potential."

"Thanks for meeting up, Doc. I know you're busy these days with your teaching stuff."

"It's alright. I was happy to hear from you. How're you doing?"

"Everyone keeps asking me that and I have no idea how to honestly answer . . .

"I think I am doing alright though.

"It's nice to get outside now that it's stopped raining . . . Dr. Greene and I are talking again, in case you were wondering."

"I knew that a while ago."

"Of course you did."

"Are you training again?"

"Yeah. I've been back in the gym for the last month. Feeling Good. Moving is good . . . You know how it goes though? Takes some time . . . I'll be back."

"I know you will.

"And the writing?"

"Doc . . . I'm trying again . . . as best I can . . . whatever that is . . . and for whatever that's worth . . . I'm trying."

"Good."

"Hey Doc?"

"Yeah?"

"Thank you."

"You're welcome."

"I'm so sorry."

"It's okay. It really is."

" No, it isn't . . . Doc?"

"Yeah?"

"I met a woman at a coffee shop last week."

"Really?"

"Yeah . . . she has a *Myth Of Sisyphus* tattoo on her ribs . . ."

"Oh yeah? Huh, how funny for you."

"Yeah . . . sometimes life imitates art— that's what they say, don't they? It feels . . . surreal."

"Well, right on. I'm glad you're trying again."

"Yeah . . .

"Hey, Doc?"

"Yeah?"

"Is it too soon to be into another woman?"

"I can't answer that one for you, Owen. Only you'll know when it's right."

"I can't tell how it feels yet . . .

"Some days the memories of Kelley come crashing like a tsunami into my soul. And the most random shit triggers it. I'll be alright one moment, then I'll hear a song, and I'll ache. It's hard, Doc, but I think now I have what you were talking about. Or at least, I am trying to."

"And what's that?"

"Faith."

"Faith in what, Owen?"

"Faith in love. Faith in trying. Faith in pushing the boulder up the mountain again. Faith in the journey. Faith in people. Faith in being able to choose my attitude in the face of the chaos. I want to believe in believing, Doc. You said that faith was what was lacking in those that are suffering through a crisis of meaning, didn't you?"

"Holy shit, Owen, I didn't think you were listening."

"I just want to say tha—hold on! Oh shit! I'm sorry, Doc, this is my mom. I'm going to take this call. I left her a voicemail earlier. . . I'll catch up with you."

"Hey, Mom . . . I am doing good . . . He's doing good too . . . So is he . . . I thought you didn't like dogs? . . . Oh yeah, Bubba is vicious . . . Never mind, Mom . . . It's not important right now . . . Listen, I want to tell you . . . I'm sorry. I bailed . . . a long time ago . . . No, I did . . . I checked out . . . I just wanted to call and say that I am sorry . . . I want to 'check back in' . . . if that's okay? . . . Church? . . . Well, let's not get carried away . . . Well . . . shit . . . I'll go to church, I guess. Just this one time though, okay? . . . There's someone there I want to try to talk to . . . No Mom, you didn't know her . . . But you would've loved her . . . I think maybe she would've liked you, too . . . I don't know . . . and I'll never know . . . But Mom? She could sing. Just like you. Boy could she sing. I miss her voice, Mom . . . She used to sing to me . . . Who was she? . . . Mom, you had to experience her . . . She was Kelley . . . Uniquely Kelley . . . She died, Mom . . . In my arms . . . I feel like I'll be able to ask her for her forgiveness at church . . . I don't know why . . . People grieve differently, Mom! It doesn't mean anything! . . .

"Don't worry, I'll tell you all about her . . .

"I think she'd like this . . .

"Well . . . I'll see ya later. Mom? It was good talking to you. Bye. Love you too . . . I'll see you Sunday for free coffee, mythology, philosophy, and singing . . . Eight in the morning?? Jesus Christ! Oh. Sorry. Eight is early though. Never mind . . . I'll be there. Bye, Mom."

"Hey, Dr. Pepper! Wait up!"

"Did I hear that right? You're going to church with your mom?"

"Yep. I figured I could set aside my pride for a few hours in order to make her happy."

". . . Owen?"

"Yes, Doc?"

"I'm proud of you. And she would be too."

"Thanks, Doc. I wouldn't be here if it wasn't for you, Sara, and Kelley . . . You know, I couldn't tell if you guys were good therapists or not. I guess it never really mattered, huh?"

"We are humans too. Fatally flawed until the end. And we are redeemed through our relationships. That's all therapy is, Owen. It's a human connection. It's someone we choose to let in. We aren't perfect—no one is. You reminded me of that."

"Well, I'm glad I did some good for that maze of yours, Doc. Shall we go to the pub? I'll buy the drinks this time."

"Wow. Going to church with your mother and buying my drinks? You really are trying to change, aren't you, Owen?"

"I'm trying, Doc. It's a journey though, isn't it? A journey with no destination. There is no end of my story. No rising action or climax. There is just life. And it repeats over and over again. I just don't want my mistakes to also repeat over and over again."

"You'll make new ones. And you'll learn from those too. That's growth, Owen. Learning from new mistakes is growth."

"Then we'll have a lot to learn, won't we, Doc?"

"Yes, Owen, we will."

The End.

Clint Haugen lives in the Pacific Northwest. This is his first novel. He also writes free-verse poetry and short stories. He plans on writing as many books as he can. You can find some of his work on his website, clintiswritingshit.com